DEAD FIX

Also by Michael Geller

Major League Murder
Heroes Also Die
Dead Last

MICHAEL GELLER

ST. MARTIN'S PRESS
NEW YORK

DEAD FIX. Copyright © 1989 by Michael Geller. All rights reserved. Printed
in the United States of America. No part of this book may be used or
reproduced in any manner whatsoever without written permission except in
the case of brief quotations embodied in critical articles or reviews.
For information, address St. Martin's Press, 175 Fifth Avenue,
New York, N.Y. 10010.

Design by Robert Bull Design.

Library of Congress Cataloging-in-Publication Data

Geller, Michael R.
Dead fix / Michael Geller.
p.   cm.
"A Thomas Dunne book."
ISBN 0-312-03318-4
I. Title.
PS3557.E3793D4 1989

813'.54—dc20
89-34844
CIP

10 9 8 7 6 5 4 3 2

For Janice Liebowitz

Fortuna

A trench coat
Bends to smell the roses
Looking obvious in a reflection
Of last night's rain.
He spies across the muddy carpet
The way it looks
For those grimacing anxiety
In the oscillating morning light
As they handicap the margin
Between a wet track and Fortuna;
Before the crowding roar
Plays its cover for the fix . . .
He knows it's waiting there
For his discovery.
Can he camouflage inside the stables
In an earshot of the inner circle,
To hear the spidered whispers
Of a lady with a black hat and a veil?
She leaves the stands like clockwork
Just as the winning horse
Corners to the lead . . .
She profiles like a client
From his early past
Who hired him as a cover
For a murder
He almost took the fall for.

Kenneth Siegelman, 1986

■ CHAPTER 1

I watched her fall.

It was October at Belmont. The overcast sky had held off the rain but the gusts of cold Canadian air that swirled worthless mutuel tickets with deserved disdain gave notice that winter was impatient.

The ninth race was a contest for four-year-olds who had won only one race in their careers. Tricia was on the favorite, Telno, and I had a fainthearted sprinter ironically named Mr. Courage.

I had gone for the lead and held it comfortably going into the turn. Then, as if on cue, Mr. Courage shortened stride and spit out the bit. That was his modus operandi and I was specifically employed to see that he didn't repeat this habit. Ken Eagle was a leading jock on the New York circuit. I was supposed to be able to make quitters run like champions. Well, not this time.

We drifted back to sixth as Tricia came from dead last on the outside. Telno was full of run. There was no mistaking the determination of the gelding as his long stride gobbled up the ground separating him from the leaders.

Tricia rode him well. She helped the horse by staying low and distributing her weight evenly. She rose up with his rhythm and urged him along with soft hands on the reins.

On past performance, there was no good reason for Telno to be the two-to-one favorite. The horse's record was mediocre, and he seemed more at home in longer races than the three-quarters of a mile contest he was entered in today. Of course, the betting public knew that Telno had changed hands and was now trained and owned by Orlando Marcano. That was reason enough to make him the favorite.

Tricia was five lengths in front of me. The two horses sharing the lead were running as a team on the inside and she chose to go around them. Telno was going easily. The crowd anticipated the stretch run knowing that a Marcano horse was like money in the bank. He would be sweeping by ma-

1

jestically, leaving the others in his wake. It happened every day. The crimson silks of the Marcano stable were seemingly invincible, defying all odds, making a shambles of the art of handicapping and throwing the racing world into a state of numbed shock.

I heard the leg snap. Over the muted thunder of three-dozen hooves the sound was a staccato pop. Telno stumbled badly. Tricia reached down on the reins to try to help him up but it was as if he had fallen down an invisible flight of stairs.

Tony Violet was directly behind her. He had no time to pull out of the way. Violet and his mount plowed into Telno and also went down. Another horse tried to leap over the tangle, its jockey bailed out, and he fell clear of the carnage.

I managed to pull Mr. Courage to a halt. I don't remember tying his reins to the rail or running to the fallen horses and riders. My eyes were on Tricia. Her small body was curled into a ball. She was lying facedown in the dirt and she wasn't moving.

Telno was thrashing about in agony, trying to get up. His left front leg was a ghastly flapping appendage of splintered bone and blood.

I had to move Tricia. She was too close to Telno. He might roll over on her or kick her with his wild flailings.

Tony Violet crawled over. His horse seemed to have escaped without too much damage.

"I'll keep Telno down," he said, grabbing the loose reins and immobilizing the doomed animal.

I gently got my hands under Trish's shoulders and moved her clear. With a small measure of relief, I could see that she was breathing. The fiberglass helmet worn under her bright silk cap had surely saved her from an even-worse injury. The helmet had been dented in the spill.

I forced myself to look at her face. Her eyes were closed, the right one puffed with blood pouring from a slash just over the brow, and there was another across her nose. Her right hand was bleeding badly and from the angle I guessed there was a break.

"Are you okay, Tony?"

"Yeah, I think. How's the girl?"

"Bad."

"She'll be okay," he said. "She's a tough little bitch."

Tricia Martin had to be tough. She took on the men at their own game and held her own. Having the skills to be a jockey was only a part of it. If you showed weakness, the backstretch crowd could grind you down for fodder. Most people knew the "tough little bitch" who could cuss with the best and give back double what she got. I knew the other side of her . . . warm, vulnerable, wary of her new success, and frightened of failing.

The ambulance stationed by the starting gate was there in seconds. They got her on a stretcher and I tried to interpret the looks on the EMTs' faces. I had talked with one of them. He was a confirmed long-shot player named George. He was usually garrulous but today he was uncharacteristically subdued.

"I'm going to ride over to the hospital with her, George," I told him.

"You're not allowed to, Ken. We'll be taking her over to Long Island Jewish. You can meet us there."

"I'm going with her," I insisted.

"What do you say, John?"

John was the driver.

"I don't care. Get him in and let's go!"

I climbed in, still dressed in racing silks, holding my helmet and my whip.

We rode through the back gate and in seconds we were on the parkway. Behind us, the tote board would be blinking the results of the ninth race and the maintenance crew would be raking over the site of the spill. Another ambulance would be carting Telno away to be humanely destroyed.

No matter how many times you see a horse go down, the impact stays the same. I had no doubt that Orlando Marcano was responsible for Telno's death. Whatever trick he used on his horses to make them win also masked their pain and their natural instinct to protect themselves. This was not the first time that a Marcano horse, seemingly in good condition, had broken down. Twice before his horses had recovered enough to win back the next time at fat prices. Telno was the second horse that had had to be destroyed.

Bob Diamond, Orlando's regular rider, had escaped injury the last time. This time, Trish wasn't so lucky. I remembered poor Telno, and I looked down at the unconscious Trish Martin.

"Damn you, Marcano! Damn you to hell!"

I didn't realize I was speaking out loud.

"Are you okay?" George asked, watching me with concern. "I want to take a look at you. You might be suffering from shock, too."

I leaned back as he stared into my eyes using a penlight.

"I know you and Martin are pretty close, aren't you?" he asked.

"Yes." It was all I could manage to say.

■ I waited in a private room that the hospital staff used to interview job applicants. It was a square little room, big enough for a desk, two chairs, a typewriter, a computer terminal, and a window with blue flowered curtains. There were a couple of plants on the desk with a green plastic container half-filled with water for the plants.

I had poked my head out a couple of times to see if I could get any information. The receptionist, who guarded the swinging doors of the emergency room as if it were the Tower of London, gave me a chilly look each time and told me that as soon as there was any information, they would let me know. That was two hours ago.

I had done my time in hospitals. Eddie Arcaro once said that you couldn't call yourself a jockey until you'd had your collarbone broken three times. My last bad spill was over four years ago. That time it was the kidneys that were damaged. Over the years I had broken my jaw, cracked ribs, and had my back broken. It was typical for someone who had been under racing tack for over twenty years.

There was a light tap on the door and it startled me. Before I had a chance to react, my friend, Gus Armando, walked in.

Gus was my height with the face of a bulldog and the tenacity to match. He was a quick-to-smile fireplug who had made the transition from jockey, to trainer, to agent, and proved the lie about nice guys finishing last. I had been a one-dimensional rider when I met Gus at the now-defunct Keystone Park in Pennsylvania. My rep, earned busting quarter horses in Texas, was that I was a great gate boy who could bring home a speedburner but who didn't have a chance with any horse that liked to come from behind.

Gus took me under his wing and taught me all he knew about pace and timing. When Gus realized that he could never be a successful trainer on the "leaky roof" circuit of minor-league racing, he took me with him to New York where he called on his lifelong contacts to give me a shot on their horses. Over the years, Gus and I had done well together, culminating with my receiving an Eclipse Award as top jockey in the country.

As my agent, Gus made ten percent of my earnings. It was more than enough to keep him occupied with the two things he enjoyed playing with most—fast cars and faster women. Our relationship had spanned three decades. He was the only agent I'd ever had and our agreement was based on a handshake given over a bottle of tequila in a drafty barn that had served as our sleeping quarters before making the big move to New York.

"What have you heard?" he asked me. "I can't get any information. They've got some battle-ax out there who won't let me inside."

"I know, I've tried a few times myself."

"How are you handling it?" he wanted to know.

He knew my feelings for Trish. We had gone out together a few times; me, Trish, Gus, and whoever his blonde-of-the-week was. The last one I remembered was named Greta.

"I think it's worse being out here than inside," I said.

Gus nodded. "I know what you mean." He handed me a small bag he was carrying. "Here, I got something for you."

I pulled out my jeans and the blue crewneck I had left in my locker, along with my regular boots. As I changed, Gus fished in his coat pocket for my wallet and two gold rings. I was glad to get out of the silks and I'd be happier still when I could take a shower and wash the racetrack off me.

"Thanks, Gus. Did you see my watch?"

He shrugged. "No, it wasn't in your locker. You're sure you brought it?"

"Maybe I left it home."

It was a special watch for me. My fourteen-year-old daughter, Bonnie, had given it to me for Father's Day. The face had a picture of Pegasus with the tips of his wings pointing out the hours and minutes. On the back was an inscription where she called me *#1 Dad*. I had worn it for luck every day since I had gotten it. It figured that today would be the day I forgot to take it.

"This was Marcano's fault, Gus. Somebody better figure out a way to stop that bastard."

"They will."

"Believe me, Gus, if they don't . . . I will!"

The door opened again. This time an intern walked in, wearing hospital greens and looking as old as my daughter.

"Mr. Eagle?"

"Yes, I'm Ken Eagle."

"Would you come along with me, sir? We'd like to try something and you could be a big help."

He walked out and I followed him.

"How is she?"

"It's Dr. Reissman's case. I'm sure he'll explain everything to you."

We walked past the receptionist and through the ER doors. They were doing a brisk business. Nurses and doctors scurried from one room to the next. Heart monitors peeped, respirators chirped, orderlies mopped, and the smell of disinfectant and ammonia permeated the air. I walked past a very old man on a gurney who moaned at regular intervals, and a baby who was having its temperature taken and wouldn't stop shrieking.

Tricia was in a separate room. She was hooked to an IV while two doctors in green and two nurses in starched white uniforms looked down at her gravely. The oldest man in the room—the one wearing glasses—came forward and shook hands with me. He introduced himself as Dr. Sid Reissman.

"Here's what we have here, Mr. Eagle. Tricia has a broken right wrist, a fractured rib, and a severe concussion. The cut over the eye was superficial, as well as the other lacerations on her face. She had a cut on the leg that needed ten stitches. Our best guess is that one of the horses kicked her and dragged her a bit. We are concerned that there may be other internal injuries and we're particularly concerned about the spine."

"There's a chance something happened to her spine?"

I thought of Trish in a wheelchair for the rest of her life, paralyzed. No, that couldn't happen!

6

"We'd like to find out. It's a possibility we'd love to be able to rule out. That's why we called you in, if you wouldn't mind trying something with us."

"No, of course not. Anything!"

"Good. She's in a shallow coma. She won't respond to us, but sometimes when these patients hear a voice they recognize. . . . Would you mind calling to her? Just call her name."

I had been looking at her from the moment I walked into the room. Her head was done up in bandages, like women do up their hair with a towel after swimming. Her usually lively blue eyes were dull and lifeless, open and staring at nothing. The cuts on her face were covered with the yellow-brown betadyne solution and she was breathing heavily through her mouth. I couldn't see the rest of the damage. She was covered by a sheet and a blanket, probably to minimize shock.

"Trish, Trish, it's me, Ken. Trish can you hear me?"

She didn't move.

"Try a little louder," Reissman suggested.

"Trish! Trish!"

Still nothing.

"Yell at her. Tell her to get up," Reissman said.

"Trish! Trish! Come on, get up! *Get up, Trish!*" I screamed at the top of my lungs.

She moved then. Her head tilted to one side and her eyelids fluttered.

"Trish, listen to me. Get up *now!!*"

You could see her trying to focus, but not quite making it.

"Tell her to move her toes," Reissman said.

One of the nurses folded over the blanket. We all watched as I yelled at her again. The toes of her right foot moved. Reissman and the others smiled.

■ CHAPTER **2** We wouldn't have seen Marcano if Gus hadn't decided he wanted to go to the gift shop to buy a box of cigars. The shop was closed, and I explained to Gus that they didn't sell cigars in a hospital anyway. That led us to the front lobby and right to

7

the fringe of an impromptu news conference Marcano was holding with reporters who were covering Tricia's condition.

"Come on," Gus whispered, pulling my arm toward the exit.

"No, I want to hear this."

I recognized Hal Epstein from *Newsday,* and Dave Siegel from the *Daily News.* The third man was from the wire services.

Marcano was a squat man, always nattily dressed, with black, oily hair and a Pancho Villa mustache. He wore colors like beige and navy that coexisted with his olive complexion. He liked gold—eighteen carat only—and loved to show off his jewelry. He wore three rings on his right hand, and another three on his left. Around his neck, supported by a heavy S-chain, was a solid gold "O" initial for Orlando. Around the track he was known as the "Big O" or "Midas Marcano." He enjoyed the press. He enjoyed fielding their questions. I had read, at least fifteen times, Orlando's explanation for his phenomenal success:

> I work sixteen hours a day with my horses. I hire only the best people and give my horses the best of everything. I spare no expense to make my horses happy. When I make them happy in the barn, they make me happy on the track. I have no magic formula for making horses winners. All I do is watch them very carefully and try to find out what's bothering them. Sometimes I put on blinkers or change some other part of their equipment. If you work hard enough and watch your horses and get to know them, they'll tell you what's bothering them. I listen, and I make them happy. I don't care what the other trainers say about me. I just do my work, and I feel bad that some people are so jealous that they will say bad things.

The truth was that he probably put in less effort with his horses than most of the trainers on the grounds. For six years Orlando had been just another trainer, winning an occasional race and looking to hold on until a good horse fell his way. For the past two years, he had been able to accomplish things previously reserved only for God.

A case in point was Bottled Water. I had ridden Bottled Water for trainer Jack West. West was as capable as they came and he had tried everything to make Bottled Water a winner. At one time, as a three-year-old, she was considered a possible stakes winner, and Jack had given her every possibility to bloom. Finally, Jack and his owners decided that they had been aiming too high with the horse and they dropped her into a high-price claiming race.

Claiming races gave every horseman on the grounds a chance to buy the animal at the price level it was racing for. It ensured that horses wouldn't steal purses by being too strong for the competition. You could be assured that if a horse was entered in a thirty-thousand-dollar claiming race, by and large that horse was worth about thirty thousand dollars.

Bottled Water won several races at this level and then tailed off with a series of injuries. By the time I rode her, she was entered for fifteen-thousand-dollar claiming races, and not coming close to winning those. In fact, during the course of the race, I pulled up on her because she was obviously hurting.

Jack West was quite happy when Orlando claimed B. W. out of that race for fifteen thousand dollars. Forget about racing, the horse was having trouble standing up!

Four days later, with Marcano as the new owner, Bottled Water raced in a seventy-five-thousand-dollar claiming race against some of the strongest fillies and mares on the grounds. Not only did she win, but she finished in a time that was only four-fifths of a second off the track record. It was just another in a long series of Midas Marcano coups.

"What happened out there with your horse, Orlando?" Epstein asked the first question.

"From where I stood, it looked to me that he stepped into a hole and that caused his leg to break. I've been complaining about the track for a week. Sometimes it looks like they got gophers living out there. I want to find out from the girl what happened. I hope she's going to be okay."

"Do you think a more experienced rider would have done better?" That was Dave Siegel.

"Well, Bobby Diamond rides most of my horses, and you don't see this happening." Orlando shrugged. "I'm not saying she ain't a good rider. I wouldn't have given her a chance on my horses if she wasn't good. When Bobby got a week's suspension I looked around and she was the hot rider, so I took a chance. Maybe I made a dumb move." Marcano laughed.

"You lying son of a bitch!" I shouted.

They all turned.

"Shut up, will ya?" Gus whispered to me.

Marcano was only fifteen feet away from me, separated by the three reporters. There were people sitting in the hospital lobby waiting for visiting hours to begin. They watched the drama unfolding as if it were a play being performed just for them.

After a few seconds of embarrassed silence, Epstein pointed his tape recorder in my direction. "What's he lying about, Eagle?"

The other reporters followed suit and pointed their mikes at me.

"Don't do it," Gus warned.

I wasn't going to listen. Telno's and Tricia's blood was on Marcano's hands and I wasn't going to let him walk away clean.

"Orlando knows damn well that there was nothing wrong with the track. That horse's leg snapped because he shouldn't have been running."

"You're crazy!" Marcano answered. "That horse's never been so good in all his life."

"That was an accident waiting to happen," I responded. "That horse has always had a history of leg problems. He needed a rest. Last week the whole backstretch saw him hobbling like a cripple."

"How come the vet passed him?" the guy from the wire service wanted to know.

Before a horse can race, the track vet checks him out at the starting gate.

"Because the vet couldn't find anything, but that doesn't mean he was sound. The horse wasn't limping then, so the vet couldn't scratch him."

"That's because he was feeling healthy and good. That's because I make him happy," Orlando smiled.

"That's because he was drugged!"

Nobody said anything. The reporters exchanged looks. It was out in the open . . . finally. The emperor wasn't wearing any clothes and somebody'd had the balls to say it.

10

"Ken, you didn't say anything about this being off the record," Epstein said.

"I know that. I'll stand by my statement."

I heard Gus mumble *shit!*

I had talked about this with Gus. Hell, everyone on the racetrack was talking about Marcano. The only way he could be performing the miracles he was doing was by drugs. All the reporters knew it. All the track officials knew it. Even the fans knew it. Any horse that Marcano started was made the immediate favorite in the race regardless of how poorly that horse had done for someone else. Bobby Diamond was winning races in bunches now, thanks to Orlando. He had been a competent journeyman jockey in the past, but because of Marcano he was challenging me and Tony Violet for top jockey honors.

Gus had always warned me to keep quiet. "You can't say anything," he'd insisted. "It's going to look like you're against Marcano because Bobby might win the riding championship."

"That's ridiculous," I had countered. "I like Bobby. Nobody is going to believe that."

"Okay, there's another reason. You don't want to be saying anything about drugs."

Gus was referring to the year I'd had to take off because of my own drug problem. It started with Ann leaving me. She had meant everything to me then, and I never thought I would get over her. I ate and drank and then took pills to control my diet, and then more pills to sleep, and then pills to stay awake. It had taken a solid year to kick my problem. A solid year to get over Ann, get over my addiction, and make a life for me and my daughter. If it hadn't been for Bonnie, I might have ended it all.

"Come on, Gus. That was almost ten years ago," I had said.

"People have long memories. It's one thing to know Marcano drugs his horses, it's another thing to prove it," Gus had warned.

Now the reporters drew me back into their circle. Marcano's eyes narrowed and he glared at me.

"You got big problems now, Mister!" Orlando hissed darkly. "Everybody knows that my horses get tested for drugs each time they run. Everybody knows that the track security raids my barn maybe two, three times a week, and they find nothing. Everybody knows that they search my car, they search my house, and they find nothing."

"If he is using drugs, how's he doing it, Eagle?" Siegel pushed the mike in my face.

"I don't know. He's got something new, something that doesn't show up in the drug tests. Whenever he claims a horse from someone, they win almost seventy percent of the time after their first couple of starts. The only time they lose is because of bad racing luck, or they run into a true champion. If anyone takes a horse back from him, the horse reverts to a cripple."

"He should know a lot about drugs. You were an addict once, weren't you, Eagle? Maybe you got too much drugs on your mind." Marcano laughed. "Maybe Tricia Martin told him she don't love him anymore. Maybe he got angry because Bobby Diamond is now the top jockey."

Marcano was goading me and in the state I was in, it worked. I lunged for him and Gus strained to hold me back.

"I'm going to get you, Marcano," I screamed. "There's a girl up there who almost died because of you. I'm going to find out what you give those horses and I'm going to nail you."

In my anger, I hadn't noticed the photographer. I didn't even see the flashbulb go off. Maybe they used special film that didn't require a flash.

At any rate, the back page of the tabloids the next morning showed Gus holding back a wild man, *me,* and the caption, of course, was: I'LL NAIL YOU, MARCANO!!

■ CHAPTER  Tuesday was a dark day at the track with the advent of Sunday racing. It gave me a much needed day off.

Ordinarily, I would still get up early to exercise someone's Stakes prospect, or to ride a special project for Joe Herrera. Joe was the Cuban-born trainer whose stable had first call on my services. If Joe didn't have a horse going in a specific race, that would leave the door open for Gus to place me on a live mount that had a shot to win.

Between Gus's ability to get me good horses, and Joe Herrera's powerful public stable, I was always within the top two or three for the riding championship. Usually it was a duel between me, Tony Violet, and Angel Cordero. This year we had Bobby Diamond battling for the title, too.

No matter how good your reputation, trainers still wanted you to exercise their horses in the morning in order to get a feel of the animal. If he liked what he saw, the trainer might want to use you in an actual race. I took a different view of exercising horses. I was checking out what the trainer had to offer. If I was pleased, perhaps I would choose to ride for him in a race. It was all in how you looked at things.

At any rate, I was taking the morning off. It gave me a chance to sleep late; seven-thirty was way past my normal waking time. I got up, read all about myself in the papers, received an *I told you so* call from Gus, and admitted to him that I had made an ass of myself.

I wondered if Ann and Bonnie would be reading about me in the Los Angeles papers.

Ann had suddenly started to take her mother-role seriously. A couple of years ago, she had asked to spend time with Bonnie and she'd admitted to me that her image required that she show her maternal side. It seemed she was being interviewed for a national magazine and her manager suggested she take the edge off her usual bitchiness by having the reporter see her together with her daughter. After the interview, they took in a show and went to a restaurant, and surprise! Ann found that she was really very fond of Bonnie.

I didn't buy the sudden reversal at first. I kept looking for her angle, but there wasn't any. Ann genuinely wanted to have a relationship with the child she had turned her back on. My first reaction was *no!* I still remembered her speech the day she told me she was leaving:

"I suppose I'm supposed to go through heartwrenching agonies but frankly, Ken, I don't feel like it. I've thought about it and I think she'd be better off with you. I love her, but not like you do. I know you'll think I'm selfish, and perhaps I am, but Bonnie doesn't figure into my plans just now. If you won't take her, I'm sure my sister will watch her for me."

That was Ann . . . Mother-of-the-Year and All-American Bitch. Her acting career was picking up steam then. She had the second lead in some Off-Broadway thing that garnered her some good reviews that led to two or three American-style Kung Fu epics; the role of villainess in a horror flick; a semiregular stint on a daytime soap; and more recently, a top-notch second lead on a network miniseries.

At twelve years of age, Bonnie was enthralled with her mother's success. Many of the preteen heartthrobs were acquaintances of Ann's. Bonnie loved to hear stories about this one and that one, what they wore, what they said. When Ann offered to take her out to L.A. for a few months, my knee-jerk reflex said nothing doing! Then I saw Bonnie's sad face and thought better of it. In the long run, the only person I'd be punishing would be Bonnie, and then I'd be as selfish as Ann.

Now, the time in L.A. had become an annual thing and all three of us looked forward to it.

Right after the disaster of Ann leaving me, I floundered around from one regrettable affair to another. It was a long time before I found another woman who really interested me.

I met Myra Walters and she was a breath of fresh air. She helped me finally shuck all traces of Ann's hold over me. Had we met at another time, perhaps it would have lasted. As it was, we parted friends, the both of us knowing we left the relationship with far more than we had when we started.

Then I met Tricia.

Tricia Martin was the top jockey for two years straight at a small New Mexican racetrack. She moved to the Northeast and established herself as a capable jockey at Suffolk Downs, and then she had a terrific winter at Hialeah in Florida where she had more money won than anyone on the grounds. Racing people whom I respected reported that if she came to New York she would do very well.

I had heard that before about other jockeys. New York is the capital of racing in North America. A week doesn't go by without some fuzzy-cheeked sixteen-year-old coming to town heralded as the reincarnation of Steve Cauthen. At the other end of the scale were the grizzled veterans of thirty campaigns, big fish in their own little ponds, who wanted to try on the name riders of New York before they called it quits. Add to this the Latins (always the champions of Panama, or Colombia, or some other place in South America), the Aussies, the English, the French . . . It never ended. Someone was always on the way to the Apple and was going to turn the town inside out. I watched them come . . . and I watched them go.

From the looks of her, Tricia Martin was no exception. She was a fresh-faced brunette, with a wholesomeness that belonged on the back of a breakfast cereal box. She was tanned a deep shade of brown with occasional freckles, sparkling teeth, and quick, intelligent blue eyes. The rest of her was on the verge of curvy yet just this side of skinny. She was too pretty to be any good. The female jocks that had made some success on the New York circuit had thick, muscular backs, arms, and legs. Trish was just too feminine. That was my first impression.

My second impression was that Tricia Martin was a bitch. I had walked over to her in the paddock to introduce myself and wish her well.

"Yeah, I've heard of you, Eagle," she said, ignoring my outstretched hand. "You're supposed to be the hotshot rider around here. Well, I'm letting you know that I'm here to do a job. I don't want your good wishes, Mister, because I'm going to be the number-one rider. You got the title, and I'm going to take it away. I don't see that as something to build a friendship on, do you?"

She walked away leaving me with my jaw hanging open like a two-dollar suitcase.

Bobby Diamond, who had witnessed the encounter, was wearing a big grin. "Friendly gal, isn't she?" he kidded.

"Do you believe that?"

"Hell, I spoke to J. C. Tanner who used her on a couple of his horses. The gal is mean, Kenny, just plain mean. He told me that a wet-eared apprentice cut her off while she was makin' a move in the stretch and after the race she went after the kid with a butcher knife."

"She looks so sweet."

"Sweet as a Texas rattler. I'm givin' that lady a wide berth," Bobby said. He tilted his Stetson way back on his head. Bobby Diamond was Texas born and bred. He never let you forget it either by his drawl or his dress.

"How did J. C. do with her up at Suffolk?" I asked him.

"He said she's the best little rider they had up there. She knew where the wire was and busted her butt to get there.

15

J. C. don't care none if there are a couple of folks that get trampled along the way. Guess neither does old Trish."

"Just what we need here . . . another daredevil rough rider." I shook my head.

"Trainers and owners just want to see their numbers on the board. The only thing that'll get them upset is if she starts crashing a few good-looking two-year-olds, then she'll be on her way back to wherever the hell she comes from."

"And where is that?"

Bobby looked at me with surprise. "Don't you read the track press guide? That's the big mystery. She won't tell anybody where she's from or anything about her past. All they had down for her was that she's twenty-six and exploded on the racing scene. You ever explode on any racing scene, Ken? The most I ever done was to pop a few times."

We shared a laugh.

"Maybe she'll become civilized after she's been around a little while," I told him.

"I wouldn't count on it."

■ I watched her ride on the reruns of races that were piped into the jockeys' room. She had what horsemen called a "good seat," just the right balance between aggressive urging and forcing. A rider who threw a horse off stride by excessive whipping or too much movement could cost precious lengths.

Tricia was polished and professional. If she got the trainers to give her some good horses, she might be a threat to win the rider's title. She wasn't going to win the congeniality award, however.

In her first week of riding she had been fined twice by the stewards for obscene language and once for fighting. She was surly and, more often than not, rude. But she was winning, and winning in racing is everything.

"I don't ride her because of her personality," J. C. Tanner was quoted as saying. "I ride her because she'll do any damn thing to boot home a winner."

I found that out the hard way.

■ CHAPTER 4

The fifth race on the card was for horses that had never won more than one race. Tricia was riding a speedburner with little heart, à la Mr. Courage. I had the come-from-behind type animal who let everything else get a long lead and then ran like the wind to either win or just miss. Clicker was the kind of horse that if you tried to rush her early, she'd just loaf along and look at the daisies. There was only one way the old girl liked to run, and that's what I was stuck with.

Tricia moved out to a long lead and I was laying fourth. At the head of the stretch, Clicker started to get serious. She went into overdrive and at the eighth pole we were second with dead aim on the leader. Tricia's horse was tiring and bearing in. I saw there was still daylight on the rail and I could gun Clicker along the inside even though Tricia was starting to drift in that direction. I made my move and was almost clear when I felt something on my right stirrup, and then my right leg.

Tricia was using an old and dangerous trick. Most riders ride "acey-deucey," lengthening their left stirrup a bit more than the right one. The reason for this is that when horses move onto the steeply banked turns, it distributes the weight so that the rider is leaning toward the inside. Tricia had lengthened her left stirrup for a different reason. Jocks hate to be passed on the inside. If a horse has to beat you, you want him to go around the "overland route," which means losing some ground by swinging to the outside. What Tricia did was to stick her leg out and lock mine, preventing me from getting past her.

"Pull your leg in," I called.

"Screw you!"

I drew my hand back and punched in an abbreviated uppercut that caught her leg mid-calf. It got the job done. Her leg was off mine, and Clicker jetted past her while I fought to keep my balance. We came in two lengths in front of Tricia Martin.

I had to wait to be weighed in. When you started a race required to carry one hundred and thirteen pounds consisting of yourself, a saddle, and occasionally a pound or two of lead bars that made up the difference, the stewards expected that at the end of the race you weighed in at about the same amount.

That requirement out of the way, and the happy picture with the owners recorded for posterity, I tore after Tricia and caught up with her in the tunnel leading to the jockeys' quarters where we were required to stay between races. Female jockeys had their own room a little further down the tunnel.

I grabbed her shoulder and spun her around. She was in lavender silks, her cap off and her luxurious brown hair cascading down her neck. The color of the silks brought out the blue of her eyes and I thought to myself that no one so thoughtless and crude deserved to be so beautiful.

"What did you think you were doing out there?"

"Leave me alone, will you? You won!" She brushed my hand away.

"Yeah, I won, but I could have gotten killed."

"But you didn't, and you gave me a pretty good shot on the leg. You don't hear me bellyachin'."

She walked past me.

"What are you going to tell the stewards?" I called after her. "They won't let you get away with that stuff."

"They won't know anything unless you rat to them, and I wouldn't put it past you."

About an hour later I was handed a note stating that my presence was "requested" in the hearing room one hour after the close of racing this afternoon. It was signed by Stewards Berry, Dwyer, and Mifflin.

I wouldn't have to rat on Tricia Martin. She'd done it to herself. She was used to minor-league tracks and hunt meetings but not too much got past the stewards in New York. The track had built-in towers populated by keen-eyed patrol judges. In addition to the side-shot taping of the races, the stewards also reviewed head-on shots of the horses coming down the stretch. Tricia's leg-lock maneuver would be picked up without any trouble.

I expected that Tricia would get at least a week's suspension. It would come at a very bad time for her. The trainers at Belmont had been watching her carefully. They were always on the lookout for fresh talent who could pilot their horses and win. The line between red ink and profits was a very thin one. A good jockey who could win a photo finish or two could mean the difference between a trainer losing his job and the stable being a success.

In addition, a new jockey—especially a female—wouldn't have the public following of a Ken Eagle or a Tony Violet. You were apt to get four-to-one on a horse ridden by Trish Martin while that same horse ridden by Violet or me would return two-to-one.

When she'd first started, the only mounts she got came from the stables that had used her in Suffolk Downs or at Hialeah. Now, slowly, the big New York outfits were starting to use her.

She had recently won a race for Johnny Long and the Pine Knot Stable. Their good-looking four-year-old, Painted Pine, was to be entered in Saturday's Stakes race. Johnny had named Tricia as the horse's jockey. The purse was worth a hundred thousand for the winner. The jockey's cut was ten percent.

Tricia's stupid maneuver could cost her plenty if she was suspended. If she did well with Painted Pine, there were other horses and other stables that would come her way.

Tricia was already in the waiting room when I arrived. She averted her eyes and I was content to thumb through a magazine until we were called into the mahogany-paneled hearing room.

The three stewards sat behind a massive conference table. Martin and I sat across from them.

Over the years I had been in this room about thirty times. It was a pretty clean record. Most of my infractions had been of the traffic-violation kind. I'd failed to keep a straight course . . . I'd whipped left-handed and bored into another horse . . . I'd failed to clear the field before crossing to the rail. . . .

There were three stewards who sat in judgment. They were Berry, an old-time horseman; Dwyer, a former jockey; and Mifflin, the ex-ambassador who was the governor's man on the board.

Mifflin started it off. "We will show the tape now," he said.

We watched as the head-on camera caught Tricia's move. It was an open-and-shut case.

"You want to say anything, Miss Martin?" Dwyer asked.

Tricia looked up defiantly. "No."

Berry was shaking his head. "I don't give a damn about

what your motive was, young lady. We won't put up with any rider tricks like that around here," he said forcefully.

The stewards were going to throw the book at her. I could see it on Berry's face, as well as Dwyer's. Mifflin seemed disinterested, but he would go along with the others for a stiff suspension. It was a matter of course for them to get my comments for the record.

Mifflin, whose turn it was to chair, looked at me. "Do you have anything to say, Eagle?" He was already leaning over in discussion with Berry. What could I possibly say? he must have thought. We all saw the patrol film.

"Yes, sir, I do."

Dwyer looked up at me, surprised. Ordinarily, the victimized party kept his mouth shut and let the stewards mete out punishment. The next time, when he was guilty, he would expect his victim to do the same.

"I'm afraid that a lot of what you saw on the screen was my fault."

"Your fault!" An incredulous Berry leaned back in the black leather chair. "How so?"

"You can't see it clearly on the films, sir, but when I went around the turn my foot slipped out of the iron. I was fishing around and trying to get it back in when I locked up with Miss Martin."

"Oh, so that's how it happened," Dwyer said. From the look on his face I could tell he wasn't buying it.

"Yessir."

I didn't look over at Tricia, but I could feel her eyes on me.

"Let's look at those tapes again," Berry said.

"Come on, Arnold. I'd like to get home," said Mifflin.

"Sir, I would hope that considering what happened didn't affect the outcome of the race, and no one got hurt, perhaps we could forget about any disciplinary action. It was an accident."

Berry was wavering. "Well, if you say so, Eagle. You were the one who was going to land on your keester."

"Let's just understand that no matter what happened out there today, it isn't going to be repeated."

Dwyer looked directly at Tricia. "Is that understood?"

"Yessir," Trish mumbled.

"Yessir," I echoed.

"All right, I'll go along with a warning," Dwyer said.

"Warning noted," Mifflin wrote it down on the judication pad.

20

"Watch those irons," Berry told me. It was his way of letting me know that I wasn't fooling him either.

We walked out to the waiting room.

I didn't expect any thanks from Tricia, and she didn't surprise me.

■ Two days later, on Saturday, she won the Commodore Stakes with a well-judged ride on Painted Pine.

She was waiting for me near my car in the Belmont parking lot. "Here," she said, handing me an envelope. She was wearing jeans, boots, and a blue Belmont windbreaker over a denim workshirt.

"What's this?" I thumbed through the envelope and counted five one-hundred-dollar bills.

"I wouldn't have won the race today if it hadn't been for you bailing me out with the stewards. I don't like to owe anybody anything. That makes us even."

I handed the envelope back to her. "No sale," I told her.

She looked at me incredulously.

I got in the car and started the engine.

She leaned over and stuck her head in the window. "Tell me, Eagle. Why did you do it? Why'd you save my bacon?"

"Because you're a talented rider, and if you *are* going to challenge me for the rider's title, you won't be able to do it on a suspension. I hope you're not too stupid to learn that you can't get away with those tricks around here. Okay?"

"Yeah . . . Okay."

"Now let me get out of here," I told her.

She moved back from the car. "I still owe you, Eagle," she said, holding up the envelope.

"Good. Buy me a cup of coffee some time."

Why did I cover for her with the stewards? I kept asking myself that same question. It couldn't be that I found her attractive. Ken Eagle didn't fall for a woman that way. No, that couldn't be it.

That wasn't the reason either why I went out of my way to say hello to her in the mornings, or find a seat next to her in the cafeteria, or finish exercising Herrera's horses and then hang around to watch her exercise Tanner's.

Ken Eagle falling in love with a foul-mouthed guttersnipe? *No way!*

■ CHAPTER  Trish did get "civilized." Her success on Painted Pine started the ball rolling. She was picking up some good horses and winning her share. The mile-wide chip on her shoulder was being whittled down.

The Jockey Standings listed her in eighth place with nine wins and a winning percentage of eighteen percent. Tony Violet was two ahead of me with twenty-three wins; and Bobby Diamond, having an incredible year riding mainly for Marcano, was barking at my heels with eighteen winners. Hector Rodriguez was in fourth place with twelve victories so Trish was only three wins off Hector and fourth place.

She would have been doing much better had it not been for Marcano and Diamond. Marcano ran his cheaper stock of horses in claiming races. Violet and I, riding for powerful stables who entered their horses in races for classier animals and higher purses, only had to go against Marcano on an occasional basis. Even in loftier company he was winning much more than his share, but in the claiming ranks—his specialty—his winning average was miraculous.

Orlando and Bobby were winning at a clip approaching fifty percent, and that was happening over an extended period of time. It seemed that no matter what kind of horse it was, once Marcano worked his magic, the animal became a world beater.

I was happy for Bobby. He had knocked around for years as a fringe rider, making a living but not really doing well. Now he was a celebrity with trainers trying to book him on their horses when he wasn't riding for Marcano. Bobby seemed embarrassed by his new success. He had no idea how Marcano was creating his "miracles." "I just sit on the horse's back and try not to fall off before we hit the finish line," he said.

For all his talk about giving Trish a wide berth, on a couple of occasions I saw them talking together and laughing about something. Ken Eagle jealous? Ridiculous!

Trish started saying hello to people, and once or twice she smiled at me as we passed going out to mount up in the paddock. Once, she was aboard a particularly canny horse who lulled you into thinking that he was going to behave and then did whatever he could to throw you. I brought my horse over to Trish's as we were both getting into the starting gate.

"Watch out for that one," I told her. "He's a bad actor. He'll go along as smooth as silk and when you're not ready, he'll try to flip you."

It was the kind of thing jockeys always did for each other. I would have told anyone riding that horse the same thing but this time I was waiting for another "screw you" answer.

"Thanks, Ken."

Was I hearing correctly?

The starting gate is the most dangerous spot on the racetrack. You're locked in a steel cage on the back of a fourteen-hundred-pound animal who could pin you against the bars and squash you like a bug. I was in the stall next to Trish's and watched her out of the corner of my eye. She was crouched low, holding the reins and set for any kind of trouble.

The horse had gone in as mildly as a tabby cat. He seemed to be waiting patiently for the gate to open. There was no sign of nervousness, no kidney sweat or washiness that signified a skittish animal. And then he tried to flip. His front legs climbed up the gate as he tried to turn himself over on Trish. She had her hands on his mane and she was holding on for all she was worth. The assistant starter standing just outside the gate was finally able to grab the horse's head and steady him down. In one second it seemed, the horse was back to its placid state.

Trish looked over to me and raised her whip in salute. "That's another cup of coffee," she said.

Neither of us won that race.

Trish seemed happy just to get off in one piece. She was waiting for me at the door of the jockeys' quarters after the racing card was over.

"How about collecting on what I owe you?" she asked me.

Did I catch a touch of seductiveness in her tone? Just wishful thinking, Eagle.

"Sure."

We went to the Argo Diner, which was far enough away from the track so people wouldn't be trying to sit near us to overhear what we were talking about. When the racing public saw two jocks talking, it signaled that there must be a betting coup in the works. Often they would strain to pick up a name of a horse in idle conversation and brag that they'd gotten the word from Eagle and that such and such a horse was a sure thing.

We took a quiet table and got to know each other better. Trish suggested that we order dinner and said she would be happy to pick up the check. I pretended to be trying to decide on what fattening and expensive dinner I would have. That got a knowing laugh from her. No one ever went broke taking a jockey out for a meal.

My weight had to stay between one hundred and ten and one hundred and twelve pounds if I was going to be a successful rider. It was absolutely absurd to think that a pound more on the back of a horse was going to make the slightest bit of difference in the outcome of a race, but weight was something trainers could control, so they insisted on that edge.

I ordered lettuce and tomato on toast and took off the top part of the sandwich, being sure to put the bread out of reach. Trish had a small salad, no dressing. We both drank only water.

Trish was in excellent spirits and I found myself talking more than I had intended. She was a good listener and seemed genuinely interested.

She asked me about Ann. It seemed that Trish liked soap operas and had read somewhere that Ann Page of "Emergency Hospital" was my ex-wife. I found myself telling her about Ann and Bonnie, and the trials and tribulations of a father raising a teenage girl. It suddenly dawned on me that I was prattling on and Tricia wasn't doing any of the talking. She was very adept at turning conversation around. I commented about it.

. She shrugged. "I guess I'm not too interesting."

It was hard to believe that this was the same brash girl. "What's happened to you?" I asked. "A couple of weeks ago you were a bitch on wheels."

"On horseback," she quipped. "I don't know, Ken." She thought about it. "I guess I was scared. That's how I relate to people when I'm afraid. I've always had that kind of attitude . . . the more you push me, the harder I'll push back."

"Except you never gave anybody an opportunity to push you. You went out of your way to antagonize people before they had a chance."

She nodded and took my hand. "Ken, I've worked for this

24

chance all my life. Ever since I was a kid, all I ever wanted to be was a jockey. When other kids were comparing their heights and rejoicing over gaining an inch, I was hoping I wouldn't grow. I've mucked out stalls, walked hots, been an assistant groom, an exercise rider, anything for a chance to be a jockey. Now I've finally ridden successfully all over the country but it doesn't mean a thing to me if I can't do it in New York. I guess I expected the worst from the trainers and the other riders. I've heard all kinds of stories about how hard it is to get started here. How the top jockeys stay together and do anything they can to hurt a newcomer's chances."

"That's just sour grapes."

"I know that now. In fact, I've gotten more help here from people in a short time than I ever did anywhere else."

I wondered if that included Bobby Diamond.

"You've gotten friendly with Bobby, haven't you?" I tried to sound breezy, conversational.

"He's a good guy. Do you know he's been talking to Orlando about me? He thinks he can get Marcano to give me some horses to ride if he has an out-of-town commitment, or a suspension."

"You don't want to do that."

"I don't? Are you crazy! What a chance that is."

"Marcano's horses are drugged. You can never tell when they're going to break down."

"Any horse can break down. At least I've got a better chance of winning with his."

"Yes, but—"

"No buts. Look, you take a chance every time you cross the street or get into a car. I'm in this business to boot home winners. You can't argue with his success. If he has a way to get them across the line faster than anyone else, more power to him."

I shook my head glumly. "You've never had a bad fall, have you?"

"I've had my share, but I'm still hanging in there."

"Marcano's a menace. He drugs horses and then he runs them into the ground, squeezing the lemon dry. When he finishes with them, they're absolutely useless."

Trish shrugged. "That's not my problem. I've got a job to do, and that's what I worry about."

I could see I wasn't getting anywhere so I changed the subject and asked her about the "mystery," as Bobby termed it, regarding her roots. I brought it up with a half-smile, anticipating a good-natured answer.

Instead, Trish's eyes narrowed and there was an edge to her voice. "There are some things I'd like to keep private. Okay, Ken?"

"Yeah, sure."

I could see she was wrestling with herself but whatever was holding her back finally won out. I had touched a raw nerve and I couldn't help but wonder about it.

The waitress set down our food and mercifully the tension of the moment was eased.

■ For the next couple of months I got to see quite a bit of Trish Martin, both on and off the track. We went out to dinner occasionally and because she had never been to New York before, I took special delight in squiring her around town, showing her the museums, theaters, and other special treasures of the Apple.

The cold, hard shell that she still showed to much of the world began to soften somewhat. The Trish I knew was intelligent, with an inquisitive mind; behind the mask of brashness was a woman a little awed by her own quick success and frightened that the bubble could burst on a moment's notice.

When Bobby Diamond was set down by the stewards because he "failed to maintain a straight course," Marcano asked Trish to pilot his stock.

She was ecstatic. "If I can pull in four wins, I'll be in third place in the standings, just three behind you and Violet."

"What makes you think we're not going to win any more races?" I asked her.

"What if I asked you politely not to?"

"Whatever you say," I kidded. But I didn't like jokes like that. I tried to be light but she sensed something in my voice. She stepped back and looked at me intently.

"Ken, is something wrong?"

"You know how I feel about you riding Marcano's cripples."

"Oh, that!" she laughed. She put her hand in mine.

"You're just an old worry wart. I think you're really nervous that I'm going to take that riding title away from you."

I was nervous, but about more than the title. Trish had become the focal point of my life . . . and I was in love with her.

That was understandable because Trish Martin was a very easy woman to fall in love with. She was beautiful, bright, and knew how to make a man feel like a man. The fact that she could be cold and elusive one moment, and all passion and heat the next, kept me off balance and constantly interested. I made up any excuse to be near her and when I wasn't doing things with her, or calling her, then I would be daydreaming about her.

Before Trish, and the short-lived romance I had had with Myra Walters, my relationship with women could be filed under two headings: One-Night Nothings and Long-Term Disasters. My luck, and for the most part my experience with fillys, had left a lot to be desired. It wasn't hard to understand, considering my limited social experience.

We had lived on a moderately successful farm in Pike's County, Pennsylvania. My father managed to turn a profit every year but it was by no means a lucrative business because of the very large corporate operations that flourished around us. The ledger sheets weren't helped either by my father's insistence that he was going to make a big score at Liberty Bell and Keystone racetracks.

His interest in horses was perhaps why he encouraged me at a very early age to learn how to ride. While other kids were tooling around on their toy scooters, I was cantering around the fields on the back of Clarissa, a gentle mare with the disposition of an old hound dog.

At the age of thirteen, it became obvious that I wasn't going to follow in the footsteps of my older brother, Mike, a strapping six-footer who was an All-State guard on our champion high-school basketball team. I measured a whisker over five-three and all the prophecies that I'd soon "shoot up like a weed" turned out to be wrong. Although I had the coordination and speed to be a good athlete, it seemed that every sport gave the advantage to the taller, beefier guys. After constant frustration and teasing, I withdrew from sports competition entirely.

My lack of height hurt me even more socially. Girls who were dealing with their own peer pressure didn't care to be seen with—or date—a boy who was shorter or the same height as themselves.

Looking back on those days, I realize now that my attitude as well as my stature were responsible for the alienation I experienced as a teenager. It didn't help either to be constantly compared with a brother who had girls flocking around him. In fact, the only date I did have in those early years finally admitted that she was seeing me in order to get closer to Mike.

It was during those dark days as a teenager that my parents surprised me one Christmas morning with an aging but genuine thoroughbred who had seen better days on the track and now was costing his trainer more in feed bills than he was returning in purses. My father had the idea that if he trained me to ride Inky's Longshot, he would enter him in races and he would win a fortune because he wouldn't have to put up with the "crooked" jockeys who sabotaged all of his selections.

One of the men who worked on the farm had ridden quarter horses out West and my father engaged him to teach me the elements of being a jock. Suddenly, I found something that I could do better than anyone else, including my older sibling. The positive feedback I was receiving from Abner, my riding tutor, and my dad, was a heady intoxicant. My father was so encouraged that he spent a small fortune landscaping a rough half-mile plot of ground into the semblance of a track.

I threw myself into the training with a dedication that I had never before shown about anything. It meant waking before dawn, taking care of Inky's Longshot, exercising the horse, doing my own exercises to strengthen my upper body and legs, and practicing specific techniques Abner had shown me. I spent at least an hour a day working on the tricky maneuver of transferring the whip (or "stick" as Abner called it) from hand to mouth, to the other hand, without disrupting my rhythm or jerking the reins. After school, there were several hours of actual riding with "breezes" and long gallops as part of Abner's bill of fare. Supper and schoolwork came next and then an eight o'clock self-imposed curfew in order to be able to get up fresh the next morning.

It was around this time that we all realized Inky's Longshot was never going to make it back to the track. Whatever competitive desire he'd once had was now long gone and even an optimistic diehard like my father, Larry Eagle, had to admit that ole I. L. would never race again.

It was Abner who suggested that I start my career as a professional jockey by apprenticing on the quarter-horse circuit. He had many friends in the El Paso area and he could place me with a family who would look after me while I learned the trade.

Abner told my father that the most important factor in American racing today was early speed. A pro jockey who could bust a horse out of a gate would be in tremendous demand among trainers and stable owners. He insisted that jockeying quarter horses, who had to reach top speed three jumps from the gate, would be invaluable experience.

At the age of sixteen, I was lying about my age and riding quarter horses on the Texas/New Mexico circuit. By nineteen, I was the leading jockey in races won and purse earnings. I was earning more money than I ever knew existed, sending home a thousand dollars a week to my parents and going through the rest like a hot knife through butter.

In a turnaround that was as ironic as it was unexpected, I had become extremely attractive to a large segment of the female population who followed racing and the scent of money. I drove a Porsche, wore six-hundred-dollar suits, and flashed diamonds on rings, watches, and bracelets. Making up for lost time, I scored indiscriminately and often, becoming as shallow and callous as the women who looked upon me as a notch on their bedposts.

My celebrity status fostered an entourage of "jockey groupies" whom I used and ultimately disdained. My dormant sex life awakened and I acquired a fair proficiency in the technique of making love, but I hadn't the foggiest notion of what it meant to be in love.

I moved from Texas to the Pennsylvania circuit, where my father finally had a chance to wager on his son, the only honest jockey in the bunch. Sad to say, I probably didn't improve his bankroll a very noticeable degree because my horses paid short prices and Dad couldn't break the habit of chasing longshots.

What my parents did notice was the change that had come over their youngest son. The shy introvert was now brash to the point of insufferability. Ken Eagle had no time for his family. There was always a woman waiting for him out in the car, or he had to run because he had an important date that couldn't be kept waiting.

Gus Armando had taken me under his wing and we left the "bull rings" and the leaky roofs of the minor leagues to try our luck in the big time of New York racing. I had almost immediate success in New York and it was here that my playboy exploits hit full stride.

Although Gus had warned me about burning the candle, it didn't seem to affect my performance on the track. I flitted from woman to woman, from affair to half-hearted affair, and through it all, if I ever allowed myself time to think, I never could shake off a feeling of unhappy loneliness. The lyrics of a popular song of the time asked the question, "Is that all there is?" and that was the question that kept repeating itself in my brain . . . and then I met Ann.

I had won the Boojum Stakes on Had To Be and his appreciative owner, Nate Coleman, invited me to a celebration party at Sardi's. Nate, who was an angel for a soon-to-open Broadway show, invited three members of the cast to join us. One of the three was Ann Page. Her real name was Valentine, but she thought it sounded too much like a stage name, so she'd changed it to Page.

That first night she told me that she knew she was going to be a big star. All she needed, she said, was the "right vehicle." Little did I know that she thought of me as that "vehicle."

The chemistry was there right from the start. Ann was like no other woman I had ever known. She was the embodiment of the class and style of New York and I, in comparison, was the stumbling country bumpkin.

I knew horses and the racing world; Ann knew everything else. "You spend every moment thinking about those horses of yours. I'm going to change all that," she purred.

I was all of twenty-four years old and I was hopelessly in love with the type of woman I had never even known existed. She was stunningly attractive and wherever we went, I knew I was the envy of every man in the room. She taught me to appreciate the theater, ballet, fine restaurants, and museums. She became my friend and teacher, as well as my lover. When we married, I knew that for the rest of eternity I would never find another woman like Ann.

It was quickly obvious that Ann didn't feel the same way about me. She became bored and restless once the novelty had worn off. She told me that she hated my hours and even the smell of horses that stuck to my clothes when I came back from riding.

Her career was just going sideways, and during the darkest time of that period, she announced that she was pregnant. Before I could tell her how elated I was, she dashed my feelings to the ground by telling me she intended to abort the child. Her reason was that her agent had lined something up for her in a spaghetti western in Italy, and having a baby then would cost her the part as well as stymie her career.

In a last-ditch effort to save a marriage that was slipping through my fingers, I offered her all the money I had in the bank, one hundred thousand dollars, if she had the child. I thought that once the baby was born, it would bring us back together. She agreed, finally, deciding she would use the money to invest in a show in which she would have the starring role.

Things weren't helped by the fact that the girl who had taken her part in the western—while Ann's show had bombed—got rave notices and the lead to a new movie for which she was nominated for an Oscar in the Best Supporting Actress category.

Shortly thereafter, Bonnie was born. Ann, once back on her feet, started searching for her elusive vehicle. The play she had invested in had never actually gotten past Hartford and I sensed that it was just a matter of time before our marriage was over.

To say I took it badly was the understatement of the century. Without getting too deep into self-analysis, I think I subconsciously believed that the loss of Ann also meant the loss of the confidence and assurance I had acquired during the time I had been with her. I saw myself reverting once again to the alienated teenager whose life was void of everything except frustration and rejection.

I lost my desire to ride and saw my weight balloon ten pounds before I decided to put a stop to the self-destruction. I spent hours in the track's sweatbox getting rid of water and also the strength it took to guide home a fourteen-hundred-pound racehorse. I switched to amphetamines and when I couldn't sleep, I bought illegal barbiturates. This cycle continued for months at a time, punctuated by three- and four-day alcohol binges.

My services as a jockey were becoming less and less in demand. I was mean and surly, carrying a chip on my shoulder with Ann's name on it, and ready to fight anybody or break down weeping at the slightest provocation.

I failed to show up for assignments—those I could still get. I even punched a horse who had beaten me in a close race. When I wasn't feeling sorry for myself, I was planning my suicide, debating whether I should do it with the bottle of Doriden I had saved on my medicine cabinet shelf, or take the messier route of blowing out whatever addled brains I had left with a shotgun.

Somehow or other, I survived.

With Gus's help, I bounced back from the bottom. I put myself on a regimen of fresh air and exercise and spent a year in exile in a trailer on Shohola Lake.

Bonnie lived with my parents, and I visited her on weekends. I came to realize that I had to fight back to win a life for me and for the little girl I loved.

In the end, I came back stronger both mentally and physically. Trainers who had been reluctant to trust me came around once the winners started coming in droves. A year later, I had my second Eclipse Award as the top jockey in the nation.

It was a remarkable comeback and I was healed in almost all aspects, save one. The scar left by Ann was deep and insidious. I began dating again but found I couldn't help holding back a part of myself to ensure that I wouldn't be hurt. I was also suspicious of the motives of any woman who seemed to want my company.

Myra Walters broke through that sorry state of mind. She was the daughter of Bucky Walters, the trainer, whose death brought us together in a bizarre twist of fate. It was Myra whose gentle understanding enabled me to trust someone enough to fall in love again.

The relationship with Myra came to an end as both of us realized it must. Had we met at another time, perhaps we would have been able to resolve some of our conflicts over the separate directions our lives were taking. Myra wanted to pursue her education abroad. I was unwilling to leave the jockey's life I knew and loved. We parted as caring friends.

When Trish Martin came into my life, I knew I hadn't felt the same about any woman since Ann. Along with her physical beauty, there was a certain mixture of toughness and innocence that really didn't make any sense unless you knew Trish.

Now, the situation I had experienced with Ann was reversed in my relationship with Tricia. I was the New York native eager to introduce the rough-hewn country girl to the pearls that were in the Manhattan oyster. I became her teacher and guide and thoroughly enjoyed her wonder and enthusiasm.

Our lovemaking was Fourth of July rockets that left us exhausted and slightly embarrassed at our insatiable hunger. I fought against it, but I knew I was head over heels in love with Trish Martin and her hard but vulnerable facade.

Her feelings for me were difficult to assess. She told me that she loved me and cared for me, but there seemed to be something that she couldn't quite express. Our relationship progressed in an erratic line that mystified and frustrated me.

We would find ourselves distant on one date, and as close as possible on another. On a graph it could be represented as going from point "A" to "B" to "C," then back to "A," then to "D," and then back to "B."

We talked about it and Trish said it was something she had experienced before. She told me she needed time. She was not used to really trusting a man, or anyone for that matter. I told her it was driving me crazy, but I understood. I had to understand—I loved her. I loved her too much not to be concerned about her riding for Marcano.

■ CHAPTER 6 I was thinking about that particular conversation as I left for the hospital. There would be no riding title for Trish this year. At the very best, Dr. Reissman told me, Trish wouldn't be able to get on a horse for at least two months. It would be six weeks before she could even think about taking the plaster cast off her wrist.

Trish's room was on the third floor. It was bright and airy

and filled with flowers from well-wishers. The largest bouquet was sent by Gus with a card that said: *Get outta there already, Gus*. Marcano had sent a floral horseshoe with a "get well" message.

When she saw me, Trish broke into a smile. She still had the bandage around her head but her color was close to normal. At the left side of her bed was an IV bottle attached to the tubing in her arm, above her head was the small rented TV.

"Don't look at me," she said in a tired voice. "I'm a mess."

"Yesterday you were a mess. Today you look terrific," I told her. "How do you feel?"

"Like somebody's been tap-dancing on my skull."

"That's to be expected with a concussion. You'll have headaches for at least a couple of days."

"There was no warning, Ken. One moment we were going fine, and the next moment I was down."

"I know. Marcano's horses don't feel any pain. They run until they drop without having the good sense to pull themselves up at the first hint that something is wrong."

"What happened to Telno?"

"He had to be destroyed," I said.

"I thought so. I was hoping that he could be saved."

"No."

You couldn't ride horses, be around horses, and not feel for them. Each had his own personality. Each became part of a stable's family.

There was a knock on the opened door and I turned to see Bobby Diamond. He stood in the doorway carrying a large box of candy.

"Hi, Bobby," Trish called.

I wasn't the only one who got the big smile, I thought.

He was wearing what for Bobby had become a uniform: the flannel shirt, jeans, denim jacket, and the ever-present Stetson. In honor of the hospital visit, perhaps, he wore a string tie with a silver bucking-bronco clip.

He flashed me a smile and focused on Trish.

"Hi, Ken. Let me run over and say howdy to the little lady."

He crossed to the other side of the bed and leaned over, giving Trish a peck on the cheek. Bobby had that aura of self-confidence and ease that I had always admired. He had been described once by Gus as being as comfortable as a pair of old slippers. I watched the way Trish looked at him.

There was no getting around the fact that Bobby was a nice-looking man. The Marlboro-man image cultivated so diligently by the urban cowboys was second nature to this Del Rio native. He had spent a lot of time on an Indian reservation with his mother, a social worker, working for the federal government. Bobby had been taught to ride bareback by the time he was seven. Like me, he had learned to bust horses out of the starting gate riding quarter horses in Texas and Montana, and by the time he'd made his way to New York, he was an accomplished jockey.

"How's she doin', Ken?"

"She looks like she's ready to ride the hurdles."

"Sure, with half a head on my shoulders and one hand. You picked a good week to get suspended," Trish kidded Bobby.

Diamond shook his head sadly. "Dumb racing luck."

"I call it Marcano luck."

"Come on now, Ken," Bobby said. "It could have happened on any horse. You never know when they're going to spill."

I wondered if he really believed that. Maybe it made him feel better. After all, he was the one riding Marcano's string and he already had had one close call.

"Trish, you should see today's paper," Diamond said laughing. "Ken looks like one of those wrestlers being held back by his manager, and Orlando is looking at him like he's gone loco."

"Really, Ken?"

"Yeah," I answered sheepishly. "I guess I made a fool out of myself. Marcano was talking in the lobby downstairs and I just couldn't stop myself."

"I didn't know you had such a temper, Eagle," Bobby said seriously.

"Ordinarily I don't." I was looking at Trish.

She reached out her hand and took mine. "Thanks, Ken, you're really okay."

There was an uncomfortable silence as Trish and I stared at each other.

Bobby broke it with a cough. "Well, I guess I have to be

gettin' along. You get better real quick. Don't forget to save me a few of those chocolates."

I knew Bobby had left. I heard the door close behind me but I wasn't really paying any attention. I was holding Trish's hand and looking in her eyes. The unspoken feelings she communicated made me oblivious to everything else.

■ CHAPTER 7

The rain hit Belmont about fifteen minutes before the first race. It was heralded by a series of thunder claps that could have knocked a sleeping man off his chair. The track, which just a few minutes ago had been a finely manicured strip consisting of a clay base and a mixture of rich loam, would now be a hard, sand-packed road with pools of collected water.

Early in the day you wanted to be on a horse who could get the lead. You gunned your horse to the rail with the knowledge that speed held up longer on a wet track. Even my old pal, Mr. Courage, might win a race on this kind of track only because as the lead horse, he could kick back mud and sand into the faces of the horses trying to catch him.

I had been on many a horse who was trying to chase a speed demon in the rain. Jockeys wore up to fifteen pair of clear goggles that could be flipped up, one by one, during the course of a race. Horses had their own windshield-wiper system in the form of a membrane that blinked from side to side over the eye. They still hated to have those clods hurtling back at them and more often than not, the more talented horses lost coming from behind on an off-track.

An off-track also presented betting opportunities. No matter what a horse's past performance, if he was the progeny of stallions in the In Reality, Graustark, or Native Charger line, you could be assured that they'd carry on the tradition of their sires and love a wet track. Other horses who were champions on dry tracks could be taken as soon as the going got damp. Even the great Secretariat had gotten upset by a confirmed mud runner, Prove Out, on a wet track.

Later in the afternoon, if the sun came out and the track

began to dry, your in-condition come-from-behind horse got back some of the advantage. North American tracks are banked to the inside so the water can drain off. Consequently, after a storm the rail is still the deepest part of the track. The track, whose sandy component in the mixture has hardened, now has more give and even gets sticky. Horses who lumber along saving their energy are capable upsets as the front runners tire badly along the heartbreak highway of the stretch.

I checked the *Daily Racing Form* and looked over the past races of the horses I was riding. One looked like a mortal cinch in the third race. He was a speed merchant that would leave everything in his wake. He would only pay twenty cents to the dollar, but this was the type of bet that people would put their mortgage on. People who did that kind of thing were called "bridge jumpers" in racetrack parlance. They would slide twenty, forty, one hundred thousand into the mutuel machines and look to collect ten percent back on their investment by wagering "to show." In a minute and change, they could make a killing . . . they could also lose it all. The one sure thing about betting on horses was that there was no sure thing.

I had seen horses, with no chance of losing, in front by ten lengths only to drop dead on the track just yards from the finish line. I had seen a sure winner in a turf race jump over the fence of the track and drown in the track's duck pond. Horses jumped imaginery shadows . . . were frightened by birds . . . tripped over their own legs. . . . Yet, on any given day, in any given race, someone might be out there putting their life savings on a chance for a quick score.

The other three horses I was riding were a mixed bag in terms of chances to win. There was a horse in the ninth race that was a complete washout, I thought. I wondered why Gus had booked that one for me.

My horse in the third won easily. I lost with the next three, coming in in the money with only one of them; and my ninth race "loser" made a shambles of his field and won by ten. He paid forty-four bucks to win and proved once again that jockeys were terrible handicappers.

I was now one winner ahead of Tony Violet who had been blanked on today's card. Cordero, who had been riding on the West Coast, was back in New York and riding in good

37

form. It wouldn't be long before he was challenging us for the riding title.

I changed and made my way to the car. I planned to visit Trish and make an early evening of it.

A gray-uniformed Pinkerton security man was waiting by the gate talking to one of the hawkers who sold salted pretzels. When he saw me, he stopped the conversation and walked over. I had seen him around before. He always had a smile and a pleasant hello.

"Nice price on that one in the ninth," he said, shaking his head.

"Did you have it?"

"Nah. I was tapped out after the fifth. I bet you made a hit, though."

"Hell, no. I was the most surprised guy on the track."

"No kiddin'? Jeez, you can't figure this game. Toughest game in the world to figger."

"You're right about that," I told him.

I made a move to my car.

"Oh, Mr. Eagle. You know my boss, Mr. Demaret. He said he'd like to have a word with you before you left today. He said he'd appreciate it very much if you'd come down to his office."

I did have some time to kill before hospital visiting hours went into effect.

"Sure," I said.

The guard, whose nametag said "Mulhaney," walked along with me.

"I can find it," I told him. "You don't have to come down with me if you don't want to."

Mulhaney shrugged. "He said to come down with you, so I better do it. He's very precise, Mr. Demaret. Do you know him good?"

"We've seen each other around over the years."

"Yeah, he's a good guy."

Demaret's office was below ground level in a winding tunnel that extended under the grandstand. We passed a large imposing door guarded by two Pinks with drawn guns. I knew that to be the counting room where the money was tallied before being taken to the bank.

Demaret's office was the next room down. My escort

knocked twice and waited for a buzzer that released the lock. I had never been down here before and I was intrigued by the security setup. Above us was a TV camera that presumably transmitted our images to another checkpoint. We came to another door that, like the first, buzzed open for us.

The inner office was large. It was carpeted in blue with modern furniture and it had a bevy of female secretaries typing on word processors or congregating at the water cooler.

One of them, a tall blonde, walked over. "Hi, I'm Nancy. Would you step this way, Mr. Eagle?"

Mulhaney nodded to me and turned with a wave. I was led to a green frosted glass door with the name ART DE-MARET in neat, two-inch letters.

Demaret was on the phone talking softly. Nancy motioned for me to have a seat on a leather chair across from Demaret's desk. She closed the door behind her and left, giving me a chance to study Demaret.

He was in his late fifties. He had a well-lined, handsome, moon face topped by a thatch of gray hair cut in a short crew. He reminded me of a movie or TV actor whose name escaped me for the moment. When Demaret looked up, I remembered the actor—Brian Keith. He was wearing a blue Palm Beach suit and I guessed in his breast pocket he had a pair of sunglasses.

Demaret put down the phone, stood up, and shook my hand. "Thanks for stopping by, Mr. Eagle."

He had a deep voice and he spoke quickly. I pegged him for an ex-FBI man . . . a Hoover man.

"Call me Ken," I told him.

"Fine, Ken. You look like a man who appreciates plain talk, so let me give it to you. I'm also not terribly fond of our friend Orlando. I think he's found a way to beat the system, for the moment. It's like a loop hole, or a technicality. A guy gets away with things like that and it's bad for everybody. After a while, the public says, 'Why bother puttin' in a bet . . . the whole thing's fixed.' When that happens, the gate goes down, the handle is off, and the golden goose dies. When the goose dies, no more golden eggs to split up. That puts me and you out of a job, and my kids wind up at a state school instead of UCLA."

He stood up and walked to a small refrigerator next to a row of filing cabinets. "How about a cold one, Ken?"

I shook my head no and watched as he snapped open the top and drank it straight from the can. He had large meaty hands and the beer can got lost in them.

"So what else is on your mind?" I asked. "You know I agree with everything you're saying. I think Marcano is killing racing."

"Sure you do, and you're not shy about talking about it to the press."

So that's what was bothering him!

He reached into his desk and pulled out a copy of the *News* with my picture on the back page.

"What the hell do you think you're accomplishing? All that happened was I got more pressure on my ass, and all my guys look like shit."

"I didn't intend—"

"Yeah, I know." He held up his hand and took another swig from the can. "I know just how you feel. I'd love to pop off about that sonofabitch, too. He sees me in the morning and goes out of his way to give me this great big hello. He knows he's rubbing my nose in it, and he's getting a kick out of it. But . . . stories in the paper about him using drugs makes it harder to nab him. The public loses confidence and he's going to be even more careful. The only chance I got to get that guy is if he makes a mistake and now, on top of everything else, I've got to worry about the Racing Board putting on a special investigator because they think I can't get the job done."

I felt bad for Demaret . . . but not that bad. "The fact is, Art, this has been going on for a couple of years now."

"Don't I know it! We've raided his barn . . . we've had his horses' feed and water tested . . . we've searched his car. And do you know what we came up with? Headaches! At first I thought it was a battery. They've transistorized cattle prods into the size of matchbook covers. Diamond sticks it on the rump of his horse, and the sucker'll run through a brick wall."

"Bobby Diamond wouldn't do that," I said.

"I wouldn't rule out my own mother if she was involved with Marcano," Demaret said angrily. "I know it ain't a battery. It's got to be some long-lasting drug, but I can't find it and it doesn't show up in any lab tests."

"Maybe if you analyze his statistics over the last few years you could get an idea—"

"Analyze! I know them by heart. Forty-six percent winners this year, eighty-one percent in the money. Sixty-five percent winners after a claim. Four-for-four on drop downs in class. Three-for-six in horses moving up in class. His average winning mutuel was two-to-one. He was eleven-for-fourteen with favorites. Six of his horses paid over ten dollars, and one paid fifty-eight-sixty. Up to last Thursday, he had seventy-six starters. He's been racing here for seven years and up until last year he never came near those numbers."

"I know that. He picks up a tired old cripple and a day or two later they're prancing around like colts."

"Well, I can't figure out what it is he's using, but I'm sure as hell going to keep trying."

"Anything I can do?"

"Just keep your mouth shut and your eyes open."

"I'll remember that," I told him.

I got up and walked to the door.

"Hey, Eagle. Did you have anything down on that bomb you rode in the ninth?"

"Not a penny," I shrugged.

"Too bad," he said, shaking his head and taking another pull on his beer.

■ CHAPTER 8

The ringing came from a long distance away.

I was driving down a dirt road that had turns just like a racetrack. Ann was in the backseat and she was laughing, and then she became Tricia. She was leaning over now to tell me something but I couldn't hear her because of the incessant ringing that seemed to be getting louder. I wanted the ringing to stop. It was important that I hear what Tricia was saying. I turned to look at her and her face became frozen in fear. "What is it, Trish? What's wrong?"

Then I woke up. The phone was still ringing as I pulled myself together, noticed it was two A.M. on the clock radio, and lifted the receiver. "Yes?"

"Mr. Eagle?" The voice was muffled, as if it was purposely being disguised.

"Yes, who is this?"

I ran my hand through my hair and tried to clear the cobwebs.

"I'm a friend. I saw what you said about Marcano in the paper."

"How did you get my number?" I asked. My phone was unlisted.

"Forget about that. Do you want to see how he does it?"

"Does what?"

"You want to see how he juices the horses? I can tell you about it. I can give you the juice. This is the only time I'm going to call you. You got to come now, by yourself, or the deal's off."

"What kind of deal?"

"You bring five hundred bucks and I'll show you how he does it . . . and what he does it with. I'll give you some of the juice and you can have it tested. You said you wanted to nail him. Well, so do I."

"I don't have five hundred dollars on me now."

"That's too bad. Forget about it then."

"What about tomorrow?"

"No, it's got to be tonight. Now! He's going to pick up his shipment in an hour."

I did want to find out how Marcano was drugging his horses. I wanted to prevent what happened to Trish from happening to Bobby or anyone else. I could get the money. I had a bank card, and I could take five hundred out from a machine. Tomorrow, I could drop off the drug to Art Demaret and have him analyze it.

"All right. Where?"

"Do you know where the bridge is in Sheepshead Bay?"

"I can find it."

"Be there in an hour. Bring the money, and no one else!"

He hung up.

42

■ My apartment was a duplex on the East Side in the low thirties. It once had been a six-story walk-up that had been converted into a fashionable co-op.

My car was in the underground garage. I was still driving my Chevy that had seen seventy thousand miles. Every month I promised myself to get a new car, but I never seemed to find the time to actually do it.

I opened the garage door with my remote and jammed on the brakes as a strong flashlight was aimed into my eyes.

"Oh, sorry, Mr. Eagle."

It was Chet, the building's doorman, who doubled as garage watchman. We had had our share of vandalism (which made me glad I owned the Chevy) and Chet had promised to put a stop to it.

"Out a bit early for you," he said.

I usually pulled out closer to four-thirty in order to be at the track by five. If this mission in Sheepshead Bay turned out to be a wild goose chase, I could get on the Belt and be at Belmont an hour early.

"I've got an errand to take care of, Chet."

"Okay, sir. Have a nice evening," he said, touching the brim of his cap.

I found a Citibank and pressed the right buttons to free up the money; then down the Drive, through the Battery Tunnel, and around the horn of Brooklyn to Sheepshead Bay.

Sheepshead Bay was a very picturesque spot in Brooklyn that featured along its wooden piers a substantial fishing fleet. I was familiar with the name because there was a one-hundred-thousand-dollar Stakes race called the Sheepshead Bay Handicap.

I had also been out past Sheepshead and Jamaica Bays on one of the fishing charters and had actually won a few bucks in the fishing pool with my fellow passengers.

The bridge my caller was referring to was a small wooden affair large enough for three people abreast. It connected the Bay with the small peninsula of the exclusive Manhattan Beach area.

I found a parking spot and waited. From where I sat I had a perfect view of anything that came over or near the bridge. I waited for over an hour . . . nothing. I got out of the car and walked over the bridge to the other side. Still nothing.

A policeman crossed opposite me as I headed back to my car. He looked at me in that funny way cops look at you late at night when they're trying to decide whether or not to question you. I was spared making up some story when he passed me by.

Out in the Bay, the boats groaned and creaked with the currents. A bright moon lit up the surface of the inky water and tipped the slightly choppy waves with tinges of white-blue flashes. I made a mental note to take Bonnie out on a fishing trip one day very soon when she got back.

I nosed the Chevy back on the Belt toward eastern Long Island and beautiful Belmont. It was three forty-five. Was this someone's stupid idea of a joke? How did he get my phone number?

■ Morning is a good time to be around a racetrack. Exercise riders—both boys and girls—wearing yellow helmets led their horses out on the deep exercise track under the watchful eyes of the trainers. There's a cacophony of sound in the backstretch. Aside from the whinnying of the horses, other mainstays of the stable are vying for attention and food . . . including cats, dogs, goats, and even monkeys. Horses are very sociable creatures and love the company of a smaller animal in their stalls. Many impossibly difficult stallions become docile with the addition of a stable pet.

That morning there was a touch of a fall chill that seemed to put all the animals on their toes. Joe Herrera asked me to take out Viceroy for a five-furlong breeze. Viceroy was being pointed for winter racing at Aqueduct so Joe didn't want me to ask him for too much today.

"Get him back in a minute-one and change."

The "change" referred to the fifths-of-a-second splits that made all the difference between winning and losing.

Viceroy was doing well and wanted the bit. I let him out a notch around the far turn and then reined him in slightly to let him know this was just practice. Herrera, stopwatch in hand, nodded slightly as we passed him at the eight pole.

Unless they were just starting out and trying to impress a

trainer, jockeys generally didn't exercise horses. I did it for Herrera for two reasons. First, I was always fighting my weight. Other jocks, like Bobby Diamond, seemed to be able to eat without putting on an ounce. I was one of those people who just had to look at food to gain. There was a time when I took it off in the sweat box. The sauna in a room near the jockeys' quarters would take a pound off every twenty minutes. Some jocks lived in the sweat box and when the time came for them to navigate their horses in the afternoon, they could hardly raise their arms from dehydration and weakness. Exercising horses seemed to help me keep the weight off so I often volunteered, to Joe's delight.

The second factor had to do with knowing Joe's stock. Horses remembered you in the afternoon if you exercised them in the morning . . . and more importantly, you remembered them. It gave me an edge to know which horse was ouchy, which was on the muscle, and which were culls or rogues.

I walked Viceroy back to shed row and noted for the millionth time the sign that seemed to be everywhere and really said it all about the business of thoroughbred racing: HORSES ALWAYS HAVE THE RIGHT OF WAY.

Viceroy would be led around a small enclosure for about a half-hour by a hot walker who would make sure that the gelding was properly cooled off after his romp. His legs would be hosed off and massaged. Then he would be washed down, groomed, and led back to the stall to await tomorrow's gallop.

Each horse in Herrera's barn was assigned to its own groom. I waited until Viceroy's groom, a black man whom everyone called Flintstone, took him in tow.

Then I made my way back to the block-long corrugated building known as "the kitchen." Every racetrack had its own variation of "the kitchen," which in actuality was a large cafeteria.

It was here that trainers, grooms, exercise riders, jockeys, and agents all broke into different groups like cliques of adolescents at a prom. Here was where most of the everyday business of racing took place. People were hired and fired, gossip exchanged, and, of course, most betting coups were hatched. Here, the *Racing Form* was king with nary a *Times* or a *Wall Street Journal* to be seen.

I ordered a cup of coffee and a slice of dry toast and sat down near the door. Generally, Joe and Gus would join me

45

and we would discuss the day's racing card. Neither of my friends seemed to be around.

I was halfway through the coffee and two bites into my toast when I spotted Herrera.

The refugee from Castro's Cuba, who had been a champion trainer in his own country and then had duplicated that feat in America, was usually unflappable. Today, however, something had gotten to him. He looked slightly lost, deep in thought.

"Joe, over here," I called to him.

He seemed to sleepwalk his way over to my table.

"What's wrong? You look like you're in a fog."

"You didn't hear nothin'?"

"No, about what?"

"Hey, Meester, where you been? It's all over the track."

"I've been exercising your horses. What's all over the track?"

"Somebody killed Orlando Marcano."

■ CHAPTER 9

Trish knew about it. I called her after leaving the track. Bobby Diamond had already spoken to her and given her the news. Diamond always seemed to be in there pitching.

I tried to find out from Trish if she had any details. The wags at the track had said that he was found in his home by his housekeeper. No one knew anything else.

"Bobby said he was stabbed to death." She sounded very upset.

"How is Bobby taking it?" I asked her.

Bobby was the closest thing Marcano had to a friend at the track. Other trainers detested Orlando for taking the horses they'd given up on and making them winners. His help thought he was a dictator, and anyone who'd ever had any financial dealings with him walked away calling Orlando a swindler. Even after his murder, you weren't hearing the usual hypocritical platitudes.

"He called me and I could hardly hear him, he was talking so low."

I sighed. It would take some time before I could sort out my feelings about Marcano. I didn't like the man, but to die like that. . . .

"I'm getting out of here by the end of the week, Ken. The doctor said I could be discharged after they get the results of some routine tests."

"That's great! But where will you stay? I mean, you can't go back to a hotel room. You'll need someone to help you with your arm in a cast, and all."

"I'll manage," she said.

"Isn't there anyone who—"

"No!" She cut me off emphatically. Her past was a door that she didn't want opened.

"All right then. It's settled. You'll be staying with me until the cast comes off."

"That might take more than a month."

"So what? Bonnie is with her mother for the rest of this school term. It's a big enough apartment. We won't go tripping over one another."

"I don't know."

"Well, just think about it then. You'd really be doing me a favor. I'm kind of lonely."

"Let me let you know." She seemed preoccupied.

Marcano's death must have hit her harder than I'd thought it would. I hung up the phone and walked to my car.

■ Chet had a worried look on his face when I pulled up to the garage.

"There are a couple of fellows upstairs waiting to talk to you, Mr. E."

"Really?"

"Yessir. They're cops. They asked me a couple of things, Mr. E. About how long I knew you, things like that. I hope I didn't do anything wrong."

"No, of course not. Someone I know got himself murdered last night. I'm sure it's routine."

Chet seemed relieved. "Oh, okay, sir. I'm sure that's what it is."

I took the elevator to the third floor. They were waiting for me in front of the apartment.

There were two of them. A thin man wearing a beige raincoat and a rainhat, and a taller man, beefy with a large mustache.

The thin man spoke first. "Hi, Mr. Eagle. I'm Detective Fusco, and this is my partner, Detective Barrad. We'd like to have a word with you."

"You have badges?" I asked, and waited while they showed me their department shields. "Come on in," I said.

They looked around, taking everything in as if they were prospective buyers. I led them to the living room and sat down with them on the couch.

"Nice place," Barrad said.

"Thanks."

Fusco leaned back. Under his coat he had on a shirt and tie.

Barrad was wearing a blue polyester sport jacket over charcoal-gray slacks. His purple shirt was a poor match, and he wore no tie. He let Fusco do the talking.

"You knew Mr. Marcano, didn't you?" He made a face. "What am I saying? Of course you knew Marcano. You were trying to slug him. I saw that picture in the paper."

"I think the whole world saw that picture," I said.

"From what I hear, he deserved to be slugged," Fusco said affably.

It was as if the two of us were sharing a secret.

"Slugged, yes. Killed, no. What's what happened to Marcano have to do with me? Aside from lousy timing on my part when it comes to having my picture taken, that is?"

"We've got some questions for you," Barrad said, seemingly bored. "Mind if I have a glass of water?"

"Not at all. I'll get it for you."

"Don't bother." Barrad was out of the chair. "I see where the kitchen is. I'll get it myself."

"Do you mind telling me where you were last night, Mr. Eagle?" Fusco asked.

"Here . . . most of the night."

"And when you weren't here?"

He was fishing for something. Chet had said they had asked him questions.

"I had to go out early to meet someone."

"Really? You went to meet someone at three in the morning? Your doorman saw you leave."

"That's right."

I was feeling more and more uncomfortable. Barrad was taking a long time in the kitchen. I thought I heard closets and drawers being opened.

"Did you see Marcano last night?"

Fusco took off his glasses and polished them with his tie. "No."

"You're sure about that?"

"Yes."

"One of the beat cops near Marcano's house identified you as being in the neighborhood," he said calmly.

I remembered the cop on the bridge. "Where did Marcano live?"

"Manhattan Beach."

"Really?"

I felt the cold hand of fear grip at my throat. Barrad was still opening and closing drawers in the kitchen. It dawned on me that he was looking for the murder knife.

"It takes your friend a long time to get a glass of water," I said.

Fusco ignored me. "You want to tell me who you met last night?"

"I didn't meet anyone. I got a call from someone to meet him at Sheepshead Bay. He never showed up."

Fusco nodded. "That's too bad. Oh, by the way, did you lose this?"

He flashed out a watch from his pocket. It was the Pegasus watch Bonnie had given me for Father's Day. I read the inscription on the back.

"Yes, I did lose it, as a matter of fact. Where did you find it?"

"It was clutched in Marcano's hand when his housekeeper found him."

I was reeling. I was being framed and the noose was getting tighter and tighter.

"I don't understand," I said weakly.

Fusco stared at me.

Barrad came out of the kitchen. "You mind if I look around the place, Mr. Eagle? I can get a warrant but if you didn't do anything wrong, you shouldn't have any objections."

"You forgot your water," I said.

"That's a fact. You don't mind if I have a looksee?"

"No."

49

He pulled a piece of paper out of his pocket. "It's just a form we carry. Please sign it. It says you gave us the right to look around."

I read it and signed.

"How do you think he got a hold of your watch like that?"

"I'm being framed, Fusco."

"Who would want to do that to you?" Fusco asked as if genuinely concerned.

"I don't know."

I was in a daze. I was trying to figure out what was going on but all I drew were blanks.

"Someone got me out of the house with a fake phone call. I lost the watch. I don't know who, or why, but—"

"Vinny, see you a minute," Barrad called.

"Excuse me, Mr. Eagle."

Fusco walked over to Barrad at my bedroom door. I heard them talking to one another. They both walked back into the living room.

"Jerry found this in your closet. It was tucked in the back, under the shoe tree."

I looked at what they were holding. It was my shirt. A simple cotton polo that I hadn't worn for at least a month. It wasn't folded neatly as all my shirts in my drawer. This one had been rolled up into a ball and hidden behind the shoes in my closet. This shirt was covered with fresh bloodstains.

Fusco brought out a pair of handcuffs.

"Mr. Eagle, I'm placing you under arrest for the murder of Orlando Marcano. You have the right to remain silent. Anything you . . ."

■ CHAPTER 10 I spent the next three hours in a twelve-by-fifteen holding pen. It was a bit short on amenities. A bolted-down wooden bench, a two-tiered bunk bed, and a commode built into the orange brick wall made up the decor. They had brought me down here after taking my possessions and printing me.

Fusco had asked me some questions but I couldn't focus. There was a kind of haze that enveloped my brain as words such as "arraignment" and "indictment" bounced around inside my skull.

Detective Barrad had put his arm on my shoulder and given me a very sincere "It's going to make you feel a hell of a lot better, Eagle, if you confess to this thing."

I told him I had nothing to confess to.

"Well, I'm going to give you a little time to think about that," he said as the uniformed cop locked the door of the cell.

The cell I was in had been built for at least two but they had probably decided that I had a better chance of breaking down if I didn't have any other prisoners to distract me. Maybe murderers were always assigned private cells. It was like a status thing: murderers drew a single, armed robbery meant a cell for two, drunks and pickpockets got crammed in four or five to a room. Maybe Fusco thought I was too dangerous to be allowed near the other prisoners.

In a way, I was grateful for the time to sort things out. I went over everything that had happened and tried to make some sense out of it.

If I hadn't been half-asleep when I'd answered the phone beckoning me out to Sheepshead Bay, I might have been able to recognize the voice. It was muffled, as if someone was talking through a handkerchief. The fact was, I couldn't even tell if it was a male or female voice.

Fusco had said that Marcano's housekeeper had found the dead man with my watch clutched in his hand. How was that possible? I believed I'd had the watch the day that Tricia fell. I had asked Gus about it at the hospital. He didn't have it with him when he brought my clothes from my locker at the track. Anyone in the jockeys' room could have opened my locker and taken it that day. Had I had the combination lock on? There were times I forgot. After all, these were people I worked with every day. I didn't carry large sums of money. The only real value of the Pegasus watch was sentimental, not in dollars. I'd have to ask Gus if he'd opened the lock on the locker. Gus knew the combination.

How many other people knew the combination? I had

never gone out of my way to hide it. Bobby Diamond had the locker to my left and J. J. Alvarado was on my right. I had known them both for years. They would never open my locker even if they knew the combination.

During an afternoon of racing, the jockeys' quarters were closed. I had never seen Marcano in the jocks' room and Demaret's security people would have stopped him even if he'd tried to gain access.

In his haste to meet me, Gus could have dropped the watch. That was really a long shot. Gus was one of those "detail" people. It was what made him such a good agent. He was very careful by nature and he very rarely, if ever, lost, dropped, or misplaced anything. Looking in Gus's closets at home was very revealing. The man had every suit perfectly arranged on hangers with matching ties and shirts inches away. His shoes were lined up in rows like a platoon of soldiers.

Then there was the not-so-small matter of how my shirt got covered with blood. Had that shirt also been in my locker? I thought about that. It was very possible that I had worn the shirt several weeks ago and had left it in the locker instead of taking it home. When the watch was taken, the shirt had been taken also. Then how had it gotten back to my apartment just in time for Barrad to pull it out of my closet?

There was a time in the "bad old days"—when I'd tried to erase Ann's leaving me with drugs and alcohol—that I had experienced blackouts. There were hours, even days, that I couldn't remember. Was it possible after all these years to have had a recurrence even though I hadn't used anything? People who had taken LSD had flashbacks years later. I felt a wave of dread course through my body. Could it be that I had killed Marcano during a blackout?

Slow it down, Eagle! Take a deep breath and blow it out slowly. You're going around in circles. You didn't kill Marcano. You know where you were every minute of the last few days. Maybe no one else knows it, but you know you didn't have anything to do with Marcano's death.

"You want to stand up please, Mr. Eagle?" The officer who had locked me in was standing at the door.

"Fusco wants to see you upstairs. Step out, please," he said, swinging open the door. "Place your hands behind your back. We have to cuff you again, that's the regs."

52

I noticed he kept one hand on his holstered gun as he snapped the cuffs on my wrists. Ken Eagle . . . public enemy number one!

I preceded him up the narrow staircase to the second floor and down a drab gray corridor. My jailer tapped on a warped brown door with the words DETECTIVE DIVISION written in black crayon. He didn't wait for a response. He opened the door and walked me to a set of cubicles and stopped by the one that had DETECTIVE VINCENT FUSCO etched on the glass door.

"Your prisoner's here, Vince," he said, ushering me in.

"Okay, Walter," Fusco said as the man left.

He motioned for me to sit down opposite him. We were sitting at a long, cigarette-burned oak table under a row of six-foot fluorescents. Behind Fusco was a window stippled with wire mesh giving a view of the street outside. There were double- and triple-parked blue-and-white police cars, a handful of unmarked Furys, and a Chevy Citation.

There was a mirror on one wall of the cubicle. I guessed it was one-way glass. Fusco read my mind.

"That's a see-through mirror. For your protection and ours, this session is being video-taped. We can't have anybody accusing us of using a rubber hose on you."

He reached in his pocket for a pack of Marlboros and offered me one. I waved him off.

"I read somewhere that I get a phone call."

"That's been taken care of," he said somberly.

The door opened again and this time a tall, dark-haired woman entered. She carried a chair and put it down.

She ignored Fusco. "Mr. Eagle, I've been engaged by Mr. Gus Armando to represent you. My name is Arlene Kirshbaum." She extended her hand. "Were your rights read to you at the time of your arrest?"

"C'mon, I told you they were," Fusco said.

"I'd like to hear it from my client. Are you familiar with the Miranda provisions, Mr. Eagle?"

"Yes. They read me the card."

"Fine. If you have no objections to my representing you, then we may get started. I have many years of experience as both a prosecutor and a defense attorney. Mr. Armando wanted only the best for you and that's why he hired me.

However, if you feel you might be more comfortable with someone else, I would understand completely."

She was waiting for my response before she sat down. She was an attractive woman, large-boned with chiseled, angular features. She had sharp, blue-green eyes and her chin tended to jut out belligerently when she spoke. She seemed tough and knowledgeable and I had faith that Gus knew what he was doing.

"I'm sure you'll do fine, Ms. Kirshbaum," I managed with a weak smile.

Her face softened for an instant. "Don't worry, we'll have you out of here in no time. Remember, you don't have to say a word. You're paying me to advise you so for heaven's sake, take my advice."

Fusco fenced with Kirshbaum for the next few minutes as he tried to establish the fact that there was bad blood between me and Marcano. He asked me about the shouting match at the hospital and then he started asking me about my feelings for Tricia.

"It must have gotten you real angry to see Miss Martin banged up in a hospital," he said, "especially when you blamed Marcano for what happened to her."

"I was very angry, but not angry enough to kill anybody."

Fusco pulled up a black attaché case from the floor and placed it on the table. He opened the snaps and drew out the white cotton polo shirt, the watch Bonnie had given me, and some stark, gruesome photos of the murdered Marcano.

"It may interest you to know, Mr. Eagle, that the blood on the shirt matches Marcano's. Is it your shirt?"

"Don't answer that!" Kirshbaum warned.

"It's okay. I know it's my shirt," I said.

"No." She shook her head. "You know that it appears to be a shirt like one you own."

"What about the watch?" Fusco wanted to know.

"It appears to be my watch," I told him.

"So it *appears* that your watch finds its way into Marcano's hand. It *appears* that your shirt, covered with Marcano's blood, finds its way into your closet. It *appears* that your automobile finds its way into Marcano's neighborhood." Fusco frowned. "You know, Ken, I really understand how you feel. I mean, this woman, Tricia Martin, is all broken up in the hospital. Marcano is sitting on top of the world. You have a riding title that's being threatened by this fellow. Hell, I think anybody might flip out and do something on the spur of the moment. I think a jury would understand that, Ken, I really do."

"Perhaps I can save us all some time," Arlene said. "Ken, did you kill Marcano?"

"No."

"Ken, have you told the detective that you don't know how your watch and shirt got involved in this case? Have you told the detective that you were called to meet Marcano?"

"Yes."

"Okay, Detective Fusco? I think that's plain English. Now why don't you drop the charges against my client. The case you have against him is purely circumstantial and an obvious frame-up."

"I really don't think—" Fusco started, but Kirshbaum interrupted him.

"Oh come on, Detective Fusco. I've read what you and your partner submitted on this case on your DD5s. You found the bank receipt from the cash machine in Ken's pocket. The time on the receipt corroborates his story about getting a call and trying to come up with the needed five hundred dollars. It also shows that Ken was on his way to Marcano's house after Marcano had already been killed."

"The coroner's report doesn't say that. The time estimate was inconclusive," Fusco answered cooly.

"What about the telephone company's report?" Arlene countered. "Someone called Eagle's home from Marcano's house according to the records. It was obviously Marcano's killer setting Eagle up."

"That's your interpretation."

"What's yours?"

"Marcano called Eagle to talk. They argued on the phone and Eagle decided he had had enough. He drove over to Marcano's house—"

"And Marcano just opened the door and invited him in as if they were the best of friends." Arlene rolled her eyes. "In the middle of the night, no less."

Fusco took the photos of Marcano and placed them in front of me. "Look at these, Eagle. Somebody got into Marcano's house. It was somebody who knew him because there was no sign of forced entry. He sat and talked with Marcano and then he buried a six-to-eight-inch knife in his belly. Until somebody can show me different, I say you did it."

"How did you know to look in Eagle's closet for the shirt?" Kirshbaum wanted to know.

"That's police business," he said gruffly.

"Come off it, Detective. You got a tip. Are you going to tell me that Ken killed Marcano and then called you with information about where to find the knife and shirt he used?"

"We haven't found the knife as yet," Fusco said.

"I'm sure you will. It'll be planted the same way the shirt and watch were," Arlene told him.

The black-and-white crime photos were spread out on the table. Something in one of them caught my eye.

"What is this?" I handed him the picture I was interested in.

Fusco picked it up. "It's a shot of Marcano's hand. He's got your watch clutched in his palm."

"I can see that," I said, "but the strap on the watch is closed."

There was a long moment of silence as what I said sank in.

Arlene got up off her chair and looked over Fusco's shoulder. "He's right, the strap's buckled."

Fusco took a magnifying glass out of his pocket and studied the picture. "Damn!" he whispered.

"Yes, damn is right. How do you explain that, Detective Fusco? Marcano, in defending himself, pulls Ken's watch off his wrist and then takes the time to buckle the strap."

"Eagle could have been wearing it loosely," Fusco said weakly.

"Look at the picture, Fusco. That isn't in the last hole, it's closer to the middle. I think you'd better drop the charges on this man before I'm forced to initiate a five-million-dollar false-arrest suit. This man is a public figure and this unwarranted arrest could destroy his reputation and his ability to earn a living in his chosen profession."

"All right, take it easy . . . take it easy," Fusco said. "Eagle, who hates you enough to try to pin a murder on you?"

"I've been thinking about that from the moment you came to my apartment."

Fusco shook his head. "There's a lot of things in this case that don't add up. I wasn't comfortable about the tip we got . . ." It had slipped out and Fusco looked embarrassed.

"I thought so. If Eagle had killed Marcano do you think he would have told somebody about it? Don't you think he would have been smart enough to bury the damn shirt or burn it?" the lawyer asked.

"I've seen a lot of very smart people do very stupid things. For all I know, Eagle could be framing himself to take suspicion off of him." Fusco tapped the table for emphasis.

Kirshbaum rolled her eyes and groaned.

"I'm not a killer, Fusco," I said softly.

He stared at me and held my eyes for several seconds.

"Maybe you're not," he sighed. "I'm going to drop the murder charges, counselor. Eagle, I want you to make a list of anyone who had access to your apartment. I don't care who they are or how close to you they are. If you get any ideas about this case, you talk to me directly." He handed me a card that had both his office and home phone number.

"You make a list of anybody who had a grudge against you, anybody who even looked at you funny. I don't want you getting any ideas that you're in the clear. You're still a suspect in my book and that means you make yourself available to me. You go on a trip somewhere, I want to know about it. Are you getting all this?"

"He'll be a good boy," Arlene said. "Cut to the chase and let us get out of here."

Fusco made a half-nod toward the door. I was up and out in a flash with Kirshbaum at my heels.

I turned to thank her for her help but she cut me off.

"Don't say anything until we're out of the building. Big brother has ears all over."

■ CHAPTER 11 It was a cool evening with a strong hint of an impending rainstorm. I took a deep breath and enjoyed breathing the air of a free man.

"Come on," Arlene said. "I've got my car parked down the block. Gus said I was to take you back to his apartment."

"How did you know you were going to get me off?"

"Hey, come on, that was a piece of cake. Fusco was just fishing. He knew all along he had a handful of wet tissues."

"I wish I'd known it."

She had a late-model Galant that she drove as if they made you pay for using the brake. We got to Gus's apartment on Madison in less than eight minutes.

Gus lived on the top floor in an apartment that wasn't as big as the Astrodome, but didn't miss by much. He had recently decided that he was going to move again, this time to a penthouse. Most of his furniture had been put in storage so we left a trail on the white llama rug and followed Gus into the dining room.

"Are you okay?" he asked, his thick black eyebrows knitting together in concern.

"I guess . . . I'm just bewildered by it all. It just doesn't make sense."

"Oh, I think it makes perfect sense to the person who killed Marcano," Kirshbaum said. "Contrary to the public's perception, the cops are happy to pin a murder on the first likely suspect that comes along. You were ripe for the plucking with that picture of you in the paper and the way you popped off against the guy."

I fidgeted in my Louis-the-something-or-other chair. It was a heavy oak with a velvet seat pad that seemed to be scientifically designed to be as uncomfortable as hell.

"I hate your chairs," I told Gus.

"At nine thousand dollars apiece, they're for looking at . . . not sitting on. I'll give you something that'll take your mind off your keester."

He walked over to the bar and brought out a bottle of Pepsi, which he poured into a glass with a flourish.

"How about you, Ms. Kirshbaum?"

"Do you have white wine?"

"Bolla Trebbiano?"

"Fine."

"You're telling me something, aren't you, Gus? Doesn't Pepsi have calories?" I asked him.

Gus swirled the brown liquid around in the glass before he spoke. "I was talking to Demaret from Security. He kind of thought it might be a good idea if you took a vacation for a week or two until things quieted down. There's no reason for you to have to put up with any abuse from the fans or anyone else."

"What's that supposed to mean?"

"There have been some death threats against you," Kirshbaum explained. "Most of the time they're meaningless, but why take any chances?"

"Death threats?"

"That's what Demaret said. He thinks they may be from members of Marcano's family." Gus shrugged. "Anyway, you can drink your soda without guilt."

"Look, Gus, I'm not running away from anything. Call Herrera and the rest of the trainers and tell them I'll be back tomorrow morning."

Gus and Arlene exchanged glances.

"I told you he was going to say that," Gus said. "Ken, you're not running away from your job. The fact is that you don't have any Stakes races coming up for a couple of weeks. This has been an awfully tough experience and a rest would be good for you."

"Sure, I'll just sit back and let someone else take the riding title."

"If you're well rested, you can come back and in three days make up all the ground you lost. You know that as well as I do. And I'll tell you something else. You owe it to your trainers to be riding with a clear head. Something like this can't help but prey on your mind. If you lose a couple of nose-finishes, the wise-asses are going to say you've got your mind on the Marcano murder. You'll start getting fewer and fewer mounts and your vacation could become permanent."

What Gus was saying made sense. Trainers latched onto any excuse to explain to owners why their charge didn't win. Horses weighed fourteen hundred pounds and more but if a jock weighed in a half-pound too high, and the horse lost a photo, it was the "fat" jockey who'd killed the horse's chances.

"All right. I'll take a week off," I told them.

Gus did a double take. "Did I hear you say *okay*? That's it? No arguments, or anything?"

"I'm going to need the time to try and find out who was behind the frame."

Gus sighed. "I knew there'd be a catch. I've already hired

someone to take care of that. I would like to see you out of New York and on a real vacation somewhere."

"Damn it, Gus! You know I'm not going to be able to relax until I know who was behind this thing. I'm also not too comfortable about having some high-powered detective agency trampling around asking questions and making nuisances of themselves."

"I promise I won't do too much trampling," Arlene said.

Gus smiled at my confusion. "Arlene Kirshbaum got her law degree from Harvard and then became an FBI agent. She's got a topnotch track record, Ken," Gus explained.

Arlene slowly sipped some wine from her glass and then placed the glass on the table. "Any objections, Ken?"

I shook my head no. "You're not the typical G-man," I told her.

"I quit the Bureau during the Nixon years. The director and I had differing opinions on the best way to run the Bureau. *C'est la vie,*" she shrugged.

There was something about the tall woman that I liked very much. I had already seen her in action wearing her lawyer's hat, and I had been impressed. I figured Gus and I could do a lot worse.

"I think the key to this thing is my locker, Gus. The only thing I can figure is that someone got the combination to the lock, or maybe I never closed it. Then they took out the polo shirt and watch and tried to frame me with them."

"How did they get the shirt back into your apartment?" Gus asked.

"No doubt Ken also had his keys in his pocket," Arlene suggested. "There are twenty to thirty hardware stores that make up duplicate keys in the vicinity of the track. All they would have to do is make a dupe and then return the keys." She took another sip of her wine.

I hadn't noticed the watch missing until I'd asked Gus about it. Had I left it in the locker or at home?

There was a long pause as we all tried to fit the pieces together. I finally stood up.

"I hope you didn't pack away the phone," I told Gus. "I ought to call Ann and Bonnie and let them know I'm okay. Then I'll call Trish at the hospital and see how she's doing."

"Ann called here earlier," Gus said. "I told her you were

60

being released. Bonnie doesn't know anything, and Ann said she wasn't going to tell her."

"There's a problem with Trish, though," Arlene said.

I felt my body tense. "What's wrong with her? Were there complications with the concussion?"

I had had a few concussions in my time. They were always potentially dangerous.

"No, she's not worse off medically. I mean, I don't think she is, anyway."

"Then what is it?"

"She's disappeared from the hospital, Ken," Gus said. "I tried calling her and they switched me around from one department to the next. Finally, I was able to get them to stop giving me the runaround. It seems that when the nurse came in to give her breakfast, she was already gone. She just walked out on her own. She didn't tell anybody where she was going, and they didn't even know she was gone."

"I spoke to her at the hospital. She must have left right after my call. She didn't say anything. She was supposed to stay with me while she recuperated. Maybe she's home sleeping."

"I tried your apartment and her apartment," Gus said. "I left messages all over the track."

"Maybe she's staying with her family," Arlene offered.

"I doubt that. My impression was that there was some deep trouble between Trish Martin and her family and it was unlikely that she'd turn to them.

"It might not be a bad idea for you to check on what happened to Tricia. I'm sure she'll turn up, but just in case . . ."

I let the words hang there. Arlene nodded.

Gus looked decidedly uncomfortable. He poured himself another drink and made a point of avoiding my eyes.

"Come on, Gus. I've known you long enough to know when something's on your mind. Let's hear it," I prodded.

Gus made a down payment on a smile. "It's just that Tricia's a good kid. I don't like the fact that nobody's heard from her. I don't like the fact that she disappeared right after Marcano got killed."

"I'm sure there's a simple explanation."

Gus sighed, "Yeah. I might be letting my imagination run away with itself."

61

Outside the sky was inky black with tinges of pink along its western flanks. It was close to five and the streets below were jammed with people leaving their offices to make the trip home. I suddenly felt very tired. It had to be the tension.

"I have to sack out for a couple of hours, Gus. Is your guest room free?" Gus's apartment could have been listed in guide books as a stopover for stewardesses.

"Coast is clear," he said, smiling.

I extended my hand to Arlene Kirshbaum and thanked her for all her help.

By the time my head touched the pillow, I was practically asleep.

■ CHAPTER  I woke up with a start, not remembering for the moment that I was in Gus's guest room. The alarm clock said 8:45 P.M. I stretched and sat up.

Gus had left a note for me on the mirror. He had a date (of course) and he'd had to leave. He wanted me to make myself at home and he'd written that he had ordered something up for me from the corner diner. Something did smell awfully good. I felt my stomach rumble in annoyance at being ignored for so long.

The "corner diner" turned out to be one of the most expensive and well-known eateries in the city. I lifted the covers off the heated plates and allowed myself the luxury of breathing in the fragrant aroma. If I had been riding tomorrow, that would have been all I could do, but since I was on vacation I grabbed a fork and dug in.

There was shrimp cooked in an aromatic sauce of garlic tomatoes and chopped onions. I couldn't place one of the ingredients until I took a couple of bites. Coconut milk! There was an exotic crunchy mix of onions, pepper, flour, and spices with more shrimp. A small tossed salad and a side of hot sauce rounded off the main meal.

There were two desserts—thankfully, both of them were in small portions, which partially assuaged my guilt. One of the desserts was a fruit mousse, light and delicious. The other was a crumbly confection of coconut and brown cane sugar. I washed it all down with Gus's own special blend of mocha coffee, which he'd thoughtfully kept warm on a goldtone hot plate.

I finally pushed myself away from the table, dashed some cold water on my face, and I was ready to take on the world.

I tried Tricia's number again and let it ring ten times before I hung up. Then I dialed it again to be sure I hadn't dialed a wrong number the first time. Still nothing.

I wrote Gus a note thanking him for his hospitality and rode the elevator down the forty-four floors to the lobby. A doorman whom I'd never seen before gave me a big smile and a touch to the brim of his cap.

"How have you been, sir?" he asked in a professional doorman's voice.

"I've seen better days," I told him as he opened the door to the asphalt jungle outside.

I grabbed a cab to my place and looked over my apartment hoping to find some sort of clue, but my quick search turned up nothing.

I called the management company and told them that I needed the cylinder of the lock changed. Instead of a human being, I got an answering machine that gave me a whole set of instructions on how to report a problem. I was to push "1" on my tone phone if the problem was electrical, "2" if it was plumbing-related, "3" for the exterminator, and so on down the line. I pressed "6," which corresponded with locks and security problems, gave my name and apartment number, and obeyed when the voice on the machine told me to hang up.

I pulled out of the garage ten minutes later and headed uptown toward the Midtown Tunnel to Queens.

In the back of my head, I had mental pictures of Trish Martin lying on the floor of the house she had rented, unconscious because of the concussion or loss of blood caused by internal bleeding. The thought caused me to press a little harder on the accelerator. I took Queens Boulevard into Forest Hills and then after a couple of missed turns, found myself on Tricia's block.

It was a middle-class neighborhood consisting mostly of one-family brick houses with postage-stamp front gardens. I found a parking place three houses away from Tricia's. Except for the whoosh of the wind through the leafless elms, the street was quiet and empty.

Tricia Martin had placed an ad in several local papers when she'd arrived in New York. She had been searching for a furnished apartment within hailing distance of both Aqueduct and Belmont. She had been fortunate enough to connect with a middle-aged couple who spent most of the winter in Florida. Instead of an apartment, she was able to have the whole house to herself.

The house was completely dark. I paused in front of the door before I pressed the bell, trying to hear any sounds inside. There was nothing. I rang the bell and then I used the heavy knocker. I tried it again a minute later. If Trish was home, she wasn't willing or able to answer the door.

There was a bay window on the porch and I tried to peer through it. Most of the window was blocked off by a blue cloth vertical blind that extended all the way except for about seven inches on the left-hand side. I pressed my face against the cold glass and tried to shield my eyes from the reflected glare of the street light behind me. I could make out general shapes of the furniture but that was all. I did a quick mental inventory of the articles in the glove compartment of my car and winced when I came to the realization that there was no flashlight.

Tricia had invited me in a number of times in the months we had been seeing each other. I knew there was a rear door that led into the kitchen. I walked through the dark driveway and wondered why I hadn't thought of parking my car there. Tricia didn't have a car and the wooden garage held the auto of the house's absentee owners.

Without the artificial light of the street lamps, the back porch was almost pitch-black. I walked up the steps, feeling my way with the handrail, and made my way to the door. I tried knocking again and then looked into the kitchen window. My eyes were rapidly adjusting to the darkness. A crescent moon and starlight supplied some illumination as I peered in. I could make out a little of the hallway that led into the dining area. It was then that I saw it.

Toward the end of the hallway there appeared to be something on the floor. It looked for all the world like a pair of legs with the main part of the torso blocked from my sight by a partially opened closet door.

I walked back to the door and tried to budge it by ramming it with my shoulder. It was made of thick wood with two sets of locks and it didn't take a genius to figure out that my shoulder would break long before the door did.

I went back to the window and tried to slide it open. It was locked shut. Glass at least I could deal with. I took off the windbreaker I was wearing, wrapped it around my fist until it looked like a boxing glove, and punched in the pane of glass just under the lock. It shattered with a sound that to me sounded like the cymbals crashing in the "1812 Overture" but in reality was probably a loud tinkling.

Too late the thought hit me that the house might be alarmed. Ken Eagle arrested on suspicion of murder on Wednesday, then arrested for breaking and entering on Thursday. I held my breath for a second anticipating sirens going off but it didn't happen.

There didn't seem to be anyone stirring in the neighboring two houses either. I thought I could hear a baby crying somewhere and the canned laughter of a sitcom coming from a TV a couple of houses down.

I gingerly drew my hand back, shook off the glass from my jacket, and then reached in to open the lock. It slid to the side easily enough, which allowed me to raise the window. I was just about to step over the sill when something hard and cold pressed against the back of my neck.

"If you move an eyelash I'll blow your head off!"

The voice sounded familiar to me.

"Put your hands up against the wall, palms against the paint." He jammed the gun between my shoulder blades for emphasis.

I did as I was told as he patted me down for weapons.

"Turn around, slowly," he warned, then: "Hell! It's you, Eagle!"

"Bobby!"

It was Bobby Diamond, sans Stetson and packing a mean-looking pistol.

"What are you doing here?" I asked him.

"Never mind that. How come you're bustin' into Trish's place?" he asked in a low whisper.

I pointed through the window. "Look over there."

"Hell, it must be Tricia."

He climbed through the window with me right behind him. We crunched through the glass and down the narrow hallway.

"Put a light on, Ken," he said as he bent down next to the body.

I fished along the side of the wall and came to a light switch. I flicked on the light just as Diamond started laughing. I looked over his shoulder.

Trish Martin's "body" turned out to be a pair of slippers on the floor next to a half-cord of wood. The fireplace was one of the things Trish liked most about the house.

"False alarm," Bobby said, smiling.

"I guess you know that Tricia left the hospital on her own this morning."

"That's why I came here to check on her," Bobby said. "I pulled up to the curb and saw someone sneakin' down the alleyway. I never figured it'd be you."

"You have a license for that gun?"

"Nope. Not a city license, anyway. I got a federal license called the Constitution. It says that a man has the right to bear arms. So where do you think Tricia is? It sure ain't like her to disappear like this."

I tried to beat back the pangs of jealousy I was feeling. I didn't like the fact that Bobby seemed as concerned about Trish as I was.

"Did she ever talk to you about her family?" I asked him.

"Ken, I got the feeling that she wanted to keep all that stuff private. If I tried to push it, she'd bite my head off. How about you?"

"I got the same response. Look, let's make sure she's not somewhere else in the house and then why don't we go for a cup of coffee," I suggested.

Together, we went through the two-story house and convinced ourselves that Trish wasn't there. There was no sign that she had come back to the house once she'd left the hospital. If Bobby hadn't been with me, I probably would have looked in the desk drawers to see if there was any clue to where she might be. With him around, though, it would look like spying. When Tricia turned up, Bobby could score a lot of points by telling her I had gone through her things.

There was one thing, though, that I couldn't pass up. A small black telephone book was on a shelf over the phone. I waited until Bobby turned his back and pocketed the book. If Tricia was okay, I'd give it back to her and take the flack. If she stayed missing, the information in the book could prove invaluable.

We left the house, but not before Bobby called a friend who promised to put in a new pane of glass in the kitchen window.

Then the Texas-born jockey followed me in his Honda to a small restaurant where we slipped into a corner booth.

I told Bobby about the watch and how the shirt had been planted in my apartment.

He listened intently and then shook his head from side to side. "I can't believe it," he finally said.

"What about it, Bobby? Do you know anything that might help me?"

"The only thing I can tell you, Ken, is that Marcano's horses in the morning are always as calm and lovable as old huntin' pooches. Then comes the afternoon and an hour or so before their race they'll be breathing fire. You remember Mr. Bubbles? Hell, that was the sweetest animal on either two or four legs. After Marcano claimed him he acted exactly the same until he stepped out on the track before his race. I've been riding that sucker for four years. He's been bounced around from one stable to another and I always seemed to get the pickup ride on him. Well, like I said, I walked up to him after Orlando saddles him and he tried bucking me off like he didn't even know who I was. It was the damnedest thing."

I could understand what Bobby was saying. Every horse has his own personality. They are remarkably consistent animals who learn something and then retain it forever. Their personalities rarely change for better or worse.

"Ken, I never saw any drugs around Marcano's barn, and you can bet that Demaret had them checked all the way down the line. I know that he had his men videotape every step a horse took from the barn to the prerace paddock. Then he'd come over himself and inspect the animal just before the horse went on the track. He'd check out all of my equipment, he'd check out the reins and saddlecloth. Marcano would be there cursing him out but Demaret wouldn't let the horse move until he'd looked over every inch of him."

"Was there anybody around who seemed suspicious? Someone who didn't belong?"

"Nope. Sorry, buddy."

I asked a few more questions about Marcano, and Bobby answered them as best he could. It brought me no closer to what I was looking for.

"Where do you think Trish is?" he asked.

"I wish I knew. She told me you called her early in the morning to tell her about Marcano."

"Yup. I was about to exercise a stakes prospect for the Hooper Stables when Betty Jean McGuire told me the news. Do you think I might have said something that set her off?" he asked, concern in his voice.

"I spoke to her after you and I couldn't tell anything. It just doesn't make sense."

Bobby had to be on the track early the next morning. We said good-bye and walked out together. We said we'd keep each other informed if we heard anything.

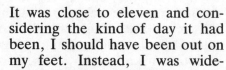

■ CHAPTER 13   It was close to eleven and considering the kind of day it had been, I should have been out on my feet. Instead, I was wide-awake with all kinds of thoughts jumping around in my head. I played out one scenario after another, balancing reason and logic against the utterly confounding facts of Marcano's death.

I would have liked to have thought that Tricia's disappearance was her way of dealing with her fall or of sorting out her feelings about Marcano. There was a time when I would have chalked up Tricia's behavior to general all-around flakiness . . . but now, that wasn't like the woman I had come to know.

That Trish's agent, Mike Westbrook, as Bobby'd re-ported, had no idea where she might be was the most distress-ing thing about her disappearance.

Mike would have to be talking to owners and trainers about Trish's health and her future plans. Agents and jockeys were inseparable parts of a team—she owed Mike an explana-tion of what she was up to.

The big fear that kept resurfacing was that Trish had been lured out of the hospital on some pretext and then the same person or persons who'd gotten Marcano had also . . .

I took a deep breath and tried to concentrate on what was real. *There are three main points here, Eagle, so let's not read any more or less into them. The first is that Marcano was killed . . . the second is that the killer tried to frame me . . . and the third is that Tricia Martin picked herself up and left the hospital without telling anyone where she was going.*

Okay, there was a fourth point, too. Trish, with a con-cussion and a broken arm, and just one change of clothes, hadn't been seen by anyone since she'd left the hospital.

At any rate, with the time nudging past eleven and me stuck in expressway traffic, there wasn't much else I could do but get home and go to sleep. Then I thought of something I could do!

I turned off at the next exit and drove back in another direction to Long Island Jewish Hospital. There might be someone at the hospital that Trish had spoken to, a nurse or a doctor who might know what had happened to her.

I kept going back to the last conversation I had had with her on the phone, when I'd told her about Marcano's death. She'd sounded, I now decided, strangely preoccupied. I had dismissed it then as part of her shock at the news, but in retrospect, I wondered if there was something she'd wanted to tell me but couldn't find either the opportunity or the words.

I pulled into the hospital lot and nestled my car in be-tween a score of BMWs and Mercedeses, all sporting MD plates.

I could see into the glass-fronted doors of the hospital and my gaze took in the surly-looking security guard whose table and chair blocked off access to the elevator banks. There was no way he wouldn't stop me, so I walked around to the side of the building and made my way into the Emergency waiting room.

The intake nurse stationed by the door was busy helping a nervous young woman fill out an insurance form. There was a long bench that extended along two walls, and fairly new straight-backed chairs made out of aluminum, vinyl, and padding. Not counting the triage nurse and the woman with the insurance form, there were nine people in the room, most of them demonstrating by grimaces or moans that they were in pain. Two large swinging doors led into the actual emergency rooms and to the left of them was a corridor that was being mopped by a black orderly in hospital greens.

I didn't have to be a genius to figure out that the hospital administration might not look favorably on someone poking around and asking questions of the staff. Add to that the fact that it was almost midnight, and Tricia's unscheduled departure had probably caused plenty of talk the night before. I figured that an element of deception was called for.

I still hadn't decided how I was going to get the nurses or doctors who had taken care of Trish to talk to me. At any rate, the first step was to get to the fifth floor, where her room had been.

The corridor led past a couple of rooms with RADIATION signs on the doors and NO ADMITTANCE warnings. I passed a men's room, and a doctors' lounge, and then I found what I was looking for.

There was a bank of three gray-doored service elevators. The only problem was another guard sitting in front of them reading the *Daily News*.

I watched as the elevator doors opened and two women stepped in. Both of them waved to the guard and called him by name, "John." They were obviously hospital employees. The guard kept his eye on the elevator until the doors closed and then he went back to reading his paper. There wasn't any real chance of getting by him without some kind of pass, and no one was going to give me one.

I knew there had to be a staircase somewhere close by and I finally saw it. It was past the elevators and the guard, John, on the other side of the corridor. Even if I could walk by the guard, the door had one of those fire-alarm warning devices; if you pushed the lever in to open the door, the fire alarm went off.

No, it would have to be the elevator, but how could I get

70

rid of John? As it turned out, I didn't have to. He suddenly got up and started walking in my direction. I quickly retraced my steps and headed back down the corridor. He was following behind, still looking at the paper as he walked. When he opened the door of the men's room and walked in, I darted back to the elevators, pushed the button to open the doors, and got in. Two men and a woman, all hospital staffers, got in with me. I got the feeling that they were wondering who I was and, for some reason, the doors of the elevator were slow to close. One of the men seemed ready to say something to me.

I beat him to it. "I wonder where John is?" I asked, nodding toward the guard's empty chair.

The fellow who had been eyeing me shrugged and pressed the close button. If he was curious about whether I belonged there, he seemed satisfied now.

"There's no security in this place," the woman sighed.

"C'mon, Tina, he's better than the other guy we had," the third man put in.

The doors finally closed and I was the first stop at five.

Unlike the main elevators that stopped in front of the nurses' station, the service elevator dropped me near an empty lounge/waiting area. The nearest room was 527 and I recalled that when Trish was here, her room had been 541. I wondered if there was any point in looking at the room. Would there be anything still there that could point the way to Trish? My best bet would be to find someone, a patient or a nurse, who might have seen something out of the ordinary.

"Can I help you?" the tall woman in the nurse's uniform came around the corner of the corridor and fixed me with a cold stare. The nameplate on her chest said MCARDLE.

"Hi, I wanted to talk to someone about my sister," I said, mustering up a semblance of self-assurance.

McArdle's eyebrows tented. "Your sister . . . she's a patient on this floor?"

"Yes, her name is—"

"Visiting hours are from twelve to two, and from six to eight. You shouldn't be here," she said sternly.

"Well, I was hoping I could see someone who might be able to tell me what became of her. It seems she checked out on her own and—"

"Do you have a pass from the admin office?"

"No, I—"

"Then you don't belong here. I'm going to talk to Ms. Curramore about this. I suggest you come along with me."

I followed along like a child being taken to the principal's office. Ms. Curramore, it turned out, was the floor's charge nurse. Unlike the battle-ax who'd stopped me in the hallway, she was young, on the very petite side, with a sympathetic face. She listened while McArdle painted the word picture of how she'd found me lurking around.

Then she nodded and said, "Thank you, Mrs. McArdle. I'll take it from here."

"Would you like me to call security?"

"No," Curramore said, "I can handle it."

The exchange between the two women was icy. There was obviously no love lost between them.

"I still think I should call—"

"I said, I'll take care of it!" Curramore said with finality.

McArdle threw back a "harrumph." We both watched her retreat to where she had found me.

Curramore turned to me. "Now, tell me what you're doing on my floor."

"Your former patient, Tricia Martin, disappeared as soon as she left the hospital. I'm trying to find out where she went."

She thought that over. "Why at this time of night?"

"It's urgent, Ms. Curramore. She might be in danger. I thought that maybe if I spoke to her nurse or her doctor they could tell me if Trish said anything about where she might be going."

"Are you a relative of hers?"

A doctor had walked over to the nurses' station and was listening to my explanation. He peered at me over the chart he was holding. He was about forty, heavyset, with an old-fashioned handlebar mustache.

"I'm Ken Martin, her brother," I lied, hoping that would give me a chance to get some information. "The family is very concerned that something might have happened to her."

"Well, Mr. Martin, I wish I could help you, but my nurses have a job to do and I can't ask them to stop and talk to you. I'm very sorry. You would also need to get permission from Barbara Muñoz; she's the hospital administrator."

72

"Maybe I could see her now."

"No, that's not possible. Everyone's gone by now. You can try again at ten tomorrow morning."

She saw the disappointment on my face. "I really am sorry," she added.

"I'm on my way down," the doctor said. "I'll take Mr. Martin with me."

I was going to say something but the doctor put his finger to his lips behind Curramore's back. I read his nametag. It said: DR. ACKERMAN.

"Thank you, Doctor. Good night, Mr. Martin."

Ackerman and I both got into the elevator. He waited until the doors closed. "You can't argue with her. She's totally set in her ways. She's the biggest bitch in the hospital," Ackerman said, smiling under his handlebar.

"I thought McArdle would win that distinction hands down."

"Gladys? Oh, no. She's a doll. Everybody loves Gladys."

So much for my snap personality judgments.

Ackerman stopped the elevator at the third floor. He stuck his head out the door and looked conspiratorially in both directions. "Come along with me," he said.

"This isn't the lobby," I told him.

"Of course not. You want me to help you, don't you? Then come on."

I followed him down the quiet hall to the same kind of lounge that was on the fifth floor. This one had two separate knots of people talking quietly among themselves.

"This is the intensive-care area. There's twenty-four-hour visiting privileges on this floor. I don't think anyone will bother you here but if someone asks, you're here to see Mr. Pollock in room three-thirty-three, Dr. Ackerman's patient. Now, what do you need to know, Eagle?"

"You know me?"

"Sure. I spotted you immediately. You've won a few bucks for me down the highway of broken dreams. I spoke to Trish, too, while she was here. I asked her for a hot tip. She told me to stick it in a toaster," Ackerman laughed.

I smiled, too. That sounded like the old Tricia.

"She's a friend of mine and I'm concerned. I called her yesterday to let her know about Marcano. It's not like her to just go off and leave everything. She could be in trouble—it could be damned serious."

Ackerman nodded.

"When I found out that she had left the hospital and no one had the faintest idea where she might be, I sneaked in hoping to talk to some other patients on the floor, or her doctor or nurse, to see if she'd said anything to anyone. By any chance did you . . ."

"From what I heard, she just had breakfast and split. You stay here and I'll check it out for you. I think Trish was Dr. Reissman's patient. I'll take a look at the charts and see if I can help."

"Thanks."

Ackerman waved me off. "Don't mention it."

I spent the next fifteen minutes thumbing through a magazine and catching snips of conversation of the two families that were assembled to support and comfort their stricken loved ones. One of the people in intensive care was a fifty-five-year-old father of four. The other family had an eighty-year-old grandmother dying of cancer. Ackerman couldn't get back soon enough as far as I was concerned.

"Ken."

I looked up and saw Ackerman motioning to me at the door. I walked over and turned down the cigarette he offered.

"This is the only place they allow smoking," he explained. "Okay, here's the scoop. I spoke to a couple of people who were on duty yesterday. A friend of mine worked a double shift and she was able to help me out. It seems that your friend, Tricia, never said a word to anyone about taking off. When they told her she might be released in a few days, she didn't seem to think it was a problem. Normally they'll argue with you if they want to get right out."

"Did anyone see her go?"

"No. She had breakfast, they came in and checked her pressure, and then she was gone. By noon, someone realized that she was gone for good."

I shook my head. "I'm back at a dead end again."

"Yeah, but there's a little twist this time."

"What kind of twist?"

"Well, this gal Jean, that friend I mentioned before, she was on call for Tricia during the night. She popped into

Trish's room about one-thirty or two A.M. and Trish wasn't there. She didn't think too much about it. There's a bathroom in the hallway and some patients would rather go out there than use the one in their room."

That puzzled me. "Why?" I asked.

Ackerman shrugged. "I don't know. It doesn't make any sense to me except that it gives them a chance to stretch their legs and see if there are people around. Jean decided Trish would be back in a few minutes. Well, around that time they had to code another patient."

"What do you mean 'code'?" I asked him.

"You don't want to get people upset in a hospital, so when you page a doctor you give him a code word. 'Code blue' means a possible heart attack. There's a 'code red' and a 'code green.' When we say we had to 'code' a patient, that means there was an emergency of some kind."

"Okay."

"Last night this lady was having chest pains and Jean was called in to help. In the excitement she forgot about Trish until much later. She decided to go back and see how Tricia was doing. As she went around the turn in the corridor near Miss Martin's room, she thought she saw Trish dressed in street clothes running into the room. Not only that, but the elevator door was closing as if someone had just gotten off. Jean walked into the room and Trish was under the covers looking like she had been asleep. Jean said there were clothes on the floor as if she had rushed to get out of them."

"Did she say anything to her?"

"No. There was nothing to say. This isn't a prison. Trish obviously didn't want her to know she had left the floor so Jean saw no reason to pursue it."

"When did your friend, Jean, say this took place?" I asked him.

"It had to be a little after four," he replied. "What do you make of it? First she cuts out, then she comes back, and then she leaves again."

I thought about it, and couldn't come up with an answer that made any sense.

"I don't know. But that doesn't surprise me. I've been having trouble making sense out of a lot of things lately," I told him.

75

■ The drive home at night took half the time it ordinarily would have during the day. By now I was very tired, having used up my store of adrenalin. I just wanted to sack out and take my chances with a new day.

The apartment was dark except for the blinking red light of the answering machine. I pressed play and heard the voice of Arlene Kirshbaum.

"Hi Ken, it's Arlene. I've got some interesting stuff about Marcano. Give me a call if you get in before twelve. Otherwise, call me first thing in the morning. I'm up and out by nine, so you have to get me early. If that doesn't work out, I'll contact you during the day. Talk to you later."

It was after twelve, and I was too bushed to talk to anyone. I didn't bother to get undressed. I put my head on the pillow and fell asleep.

■ CHAPTER 14 I automatically woke up at four-thirty, but forced myself to go back to sleep after setting the alarm for eight. After a force-of-habit breakfast of orange juice (half a glass) and one slice of dry toast, I tried Trish's house (no answer), then dialed Arlene Kirshbaum, who answered on the first ring.

"Hi, I tried getting you most of the night," she said after she heard my voice.

I told her about my soiré at Trish's and the events at the hospital.

"Interesting," was her one-word reply. "That was just about the same time you were called to go to Marcano's."

"I doubt there was a tie-in," I said.

"Probably not." She didn't sound too sure. "Anyway, let me tell you about your friend Marcano. It seems the Big O was heavily in debt. He was in hock all the way up to the gold-rimmed reading glasses they found in his pocket."

"How could that be? He was the most successful trainer on the grounds."

"He forgot a small matter of paying taxes for the years nineteen-eighty through eighty-five. Our uncle with the white beard and funny hat frowns on that kind of behavior. Every time Orlando won a race, a good portion of the money supposedly went into federal coffers. Add the fact that the man believed in pampering himself at every turn, and throw in the name of a character known around the racetrack as Bath Beach Frankie, and if you're Orlando Marcano, you've got a big financial problem."

"I know Frankie," I said. Bath Beach Frankie was a well-connected shylock who catered to the racing trade.

"As the late Willie Sutton used to say, 'You go where the money is.'"

I thought over Arlene's scoop.

"I'm going to have a talk with Frankie. Maybe I can get a line on Orlando and in turn, find out who tried to frame me."

"Maybe you should just take it easy and let me dig," she suggested.

"No, Arlene, I'm driving myself crazy. I've got to do something to keep my mind off Tricia."

There was a pause on the other end as Arlene tried to muster an argument to talk me out of getting involved.

"All right, but be careful," she finally said. "Fusco feels a little embarrassed about you walking out of the station house. He wouldn't mind coming up with a charge that he could make stick. By the by, did you ever make up that list he asked for?"

"You mean that 'I hate Ken Eagle' list? Well, I've thought about it and to tell you the truth, I just can't think of anyone that disliked me that much and who also knew Marcano."

"All right, Ken. You keep thinking. It might be a good idea for us to compare notes. I have an office on Broadway near the State Building on Worth. Can you meet me at six?"

I told her I could and copied down the exact address. I remembered the phone book I had taken from Trish's house and told Arlene about it.

"Bring it along," she said, "it might be helpful."

I hung up and looked for the small, black leatherbound book. It contained thirty numbers in all. One-third of them were New York service businesses. There was a cleaner, hairdresser, a bunch of fast-food takeout places, a neighborhood grocery, a fruit store, and a pharmacy. There were also seven numbers and names I recognized, including my own, Diamond, Marcano, Mike Westbrook, and four other people Trish knew from the track.

It was the last dozen or so numbers, however, that I found interesting. They all had a 404 area code, which I looked up and found was a rural Georgia exchange. These people were part of the past Trish had chosen to bury.

I was torn by an inner conflict. Should I respect Trish's privacy and forget I had those numbers? Another part of me argued that Trish might be in trouble and I had to do something to help her.

Before I could change my mind, I took the phone and dialed the number of Oliver and Gloria Pusey. It rang five times before someone answered.

"Yeass?"

"Hello, I'm calling from New York. My name is Ken Eagle and I'm a friend of Tricia Martin's. I wonder if you could help me."

"Sure, if'n I can," she said in a smooth Georgia accent.

"I'm trying to locate Tricia."

"Who?"

"Tricia Martin."

"Sorry, I don' know any Tricia Martin."

"Is this the Pusey residence?"

"Yeass, it is."

"Are you Gloria Pusey?"

"I sure am, but I don' know anybody named Tricia."

"Perhaps your husband . . ."

"Well, if yo'll hold on, I'll ask him." There was a rustling on the line. "Ollie honey, you know a gal named Tricia Martin? A fella from New York is on the wire askin' about her. . . . No, Mr. Eagle, he don' know her either. Are you sure you've got the right Puseys? We got kinfolk in Rome named Jess and Steve."

"No, that's okay. It's my mistake."

I called the rest of the numbers. Half of them didn't answer or directed me to leave a message on the machine. The other people I talked to, like the Puseys, had never heard of Tricia Martin.

I tucked the telephone book into my pocket in the hope that maybe Arlene could figure out what was going on. If Tricia had changed her name legally, then perhaps Arlene or her contacts could tap into the government computers and find out her original family name.

■ I knew where to find Bath Beach Frankie. Every morning at precisely nine A.M. his gray limousine pulled into the same parking space under an overhanging elm in the Aqueduct parking lot. It was here that Frankie and his lieutenant, a hulk of a man everyone called Homeboy Looie, held court.

It was rumored that you could borrow anything you needed from Frankie, up to a cool million, as long as you could dig up the nominal fifty-points-a-week interest.

I parked my car next to the block-long Continental and waited for the chauffeur to walk over to me.

"Ken Eagle." He registered surprise at seeing me. "You here to see Bath Beach?" he asked.

"If he can spare a few minutes."

"You want to do business?"

"I have to ask him something about Marcano."

I saw the chauffeur's eyes spark for a brief second. He was a compact five-feet-nine, no neck, with greasy black hair.

"I gotta check with Bath Beach. You wanna step out of the car?"

I got out.

"Sorry, Eagle, but we got a lot of very weird-thinking people around. Frankie's orders." He patted me down for weapons.

"I understand."

"Stay here a sec."

He tapped on the rear window of the car and it rolled down an inch. The windows were darkly tinted and there was no way to see inside. The chauffeur nodded and called me over. He opened the door for me and I climbed in.

Although I had known Bath Beach Frankie as I knew many other track characters, through mutual acquaintances and reputation, this was the first time I had ever been to Frankie's "office."

The spacious rear compartment was separated from the

driver by thick plexiglass, probably bulletproof. Frankie had a bar, TV, stereo, telephone, and a fold-down marble table, which now held a silver coffeepot and fine china cups and saucers. There were two black leather bench seats. I sat down and sank into the plush foam rubber. Frankie and Homeboy sat across from me.

"Some coffee, Eagle?" Frankie offered.

He was a studious-looking man with thick glasses and an acne-scarred complexion. Homeboy was half his age, about twenty-five. He had a big head with uneven and missing teeth that made him look like a Halloween jack-o-lantern. He was Frankie's muscle and he fit the part. Even sitting, he was imposing, with forearms and biceps that stretched the material of his black polo. Bath Beach, though not a small man, looked small next to Homeboy.

"Do you know Mr. Eagle, Looie?" Frank asked his side-kick.

"I seen him around," Homeboy grunted.

"I'll pass on the coffee, Frankie," I said.

"Okay. You don't mind if we have some, then."

He poured and handed a cup and saucer to Homeboy. It was amazing how the cup seemed to get lost in his big hand.

As he took it from Frankie, he spilled it on himself. "Damn! Why can't we drink from a container. I hate this cup shit!"

Frankie chuckled. "You can take the boy out of the Lower East Side, but you can't take the Lower East Side out of the boy. Eh, Eagle?"

"Whatever you say, Frankie," I said, being amiable.

The loanshark leaned back and took a sip from his cup. "You told Joey that you had a question about Marcano. Didn't I hear somewhere that the cops got you on that little number?"

"They made a mistake."

"I'm glad to hear that, because Orlando was a dear friend of mine."

"Then you're in very select company," I said.

Frankie smiled. His mouth was like an open wound with teeth. "You're right. He wasn't a dear friend. In fact, I hated the bum." Frankie started laughing again. I must have caught him on a good day.

"I heard he owed you money."

Bath Beach nodded. "You heard right, Ken. Two hundred big ones. His death makes it hard to collect. How about you get me that money, Homeboy?"

"That man pay the loan, or I break his bone," Homeboy said seriously.

Bath Beach tilted his head at Homeboy. "He loves that rhyme shit. So what makes you interested in the late Orlando Marcano?"

"Somebody tried to stick me with the murder and that doesn't sit well. Do you know anybody who'd want to kill him?"

"There isn't a soul on the track who could stand the guy. What did your lady friend see in him?"

"Trish?"

"Yah, the Martin girl. They were a hot item for a while."

I sat up in my chair. "What are you talking about, Frankie? Trish never dated Marcano. He gave her a couple of mounts, that's all."

"I'll say he gave her a mount. I wouldn't mind mounting her myself. Uh-oh, Eagle's getting angry. Come on Ken, you didn't think that girl was the Virgin Mary, did you?"

"You're full of it, Frankie," I snapped.

Homebody put his hand out menacingly. "Watch it, Jack! . . . I'm dressed in black and I don't step back. Better cool down . . . if you want to stay aroun'."

"Hey, Ken," Frankie shrugged. "What's it mean to me? I got no reason to lie to you."

It was possible, of course. I hadn't been involved with Tricia when she first came to New York. As a newcomer on the scene she would have wanted to be introduced to the leading trainer, Orlando Marcano. And Marcano was known as a man who had an eye for the ladies. Wouldn't Tricia have mentioned something if she and Marcano had been seeing each other? I couldn't be sure. There seemed to be two Tricias. One was a frightened, unsure, young woman, open and caring. The other was a cold, hard, calculating person with a mysterious past who acted erratically.

A lot of Tricia's behavior, I knew, had to do with the innate sexism of the racetrack. As in any industry dominated by men, a woman, particularly a pretty woman, could be given a rough time. Where I might have a brief conversation with a trainer like Marcano, that same conversation between Trish and Orlando would be viewed by some as Tricia playing up to the trainer. There wasn't a woman on the track who'd achieved some success who wasn't rumored to have achieved that success by sleeping with an influential man. Every female jockey, according to those sources, was going to bed with an owner or trainer.

Bath Beach Frankie would have been one of the first to spread that kind of rumor. Whatever the truth about the situation, I wasn't going to show how I felt to the loan shark and his goon.

"I know a lot of people didn't like Marcano, I was one of them, but who would go so far as to turn dislike into murder?"

"I got no idea. I'm just a businessman trying to earn a living," Frankie said with a straight face.

"Why did Marcano need money from you? He was making it hand over fist."

"He had trouble with the feds. They were skimming his purses and watching him at the betting windows. He also needed a stake for some big deal that he had cooked up."

"Like what?"

"Sorry, that's privileged information. I got to respect my clients, even if they're dead."

"You're a prince, Frankie," I told him. "How come you don't seem upset that Marcano died and you didn't collect your money?"

"I got back my principle; he was just paying off the weekly juice. So what do you say, Eagle. You want to do business?"

"No, I just needed some information."

"Well, I'm always glad to help a fellow horseman. We track people have to stick together. You're going to have to excuse me now since me and Homeboy have a few things to talk over."

I let myself out of the limo and into the blinding sunshine of the crisp fall day. I didn't like Frankie, but he didn't put a gun to your head and make you borrow money from him. Nobody went to a loan shark because they mistook him for a banker. As far as helping me, my visit to Frankie's "office" raised more questions than it had answered.

I spent the next hour walking along the backstretch and asking about Tricia. I didn't expect to make any progress, and I was right.

At one point Bobby Diamond approached me and the look on his face told me that he had been just as frustrated as me in trying to find Trish.

"You haven't heard anything, have you?" he asked me.

"No, I was hoping you had."

We both leaned against the track rail and watched a two-year-old filly breeze a quarter-of-a-mile in fast time. This was a good one, gliding effortlessly with a perfect gait. The horse pulled up and the owner and his wife came over to the animal. The exercise boy was talking to them with obvious excitement, probably telling them that the filly would win the Kentucky Derby. For now, the animal could be "any kind." She could be compared to Genuine Risk, Honest Pleasure, or even Ruffian. What would happen later when the horse would be asked to show her stuff on the track . . . well, that could be an entirely different matter. If you got by the bowed tendons, the split hoofs, the colic, the cribbing, the equine fevers, the bleeding, the rundown inflammations, the incompetent trainers and grooms, then she might have a chance to win a race or two. Or, she could be, in track parlance, a "morning glory." They were great to look at, and wonderful in their morning workouts, but they couldn't run a lick with money on the line.

The owner patted the young horse's head. Horses, not Maltese falcons, were the real stuff that dreams are made of. Hope always springs eternal on the backstretch. It was said that no one ever committed suicide at a racetrack because there was always a new crop of foals coming along that might change one's life.

I turned around and looked at Diamond. "Bobby, was Marcano going out with Trish?"

He didn't answer at first, and I thought he didn't hear me.

"I can't say for sure, Ken, but they seemed to be a lot closer than they let on to people," he said finally. "I remember she once called him and I answered the phone at the barn. You know how Marcano is . . . was. You know what I mean, a real loudmouth and all. When he got on the phone with Trish, he got very quiet. He held his hand over the mouthpiece and was whispering for at least a half-hour."

"That could have been business," I said.

"It could have," Bobby agreed.

It was obvious, though, that he didn't think so.

Bobby took off for the barn area and I traded pleasantries with some old friends. Then I headed for the area below the grandstand to talk to the head of Security, Art Demaret.

It had been Demaret who had been watching Marcano the closest over the past year. It stood to reason that Art might be able to shed some light on who would have wanted Marcano dead, and who would have tried to make me the fall guy.

As I descended to the Security area beneath the gray concrete stands, I heard the crowd roaring as the horses in the First Race neared the finish line. It was a strange sound for me.

When you were riding, you heard the sound of hooves and the yelling of the other riders as they urged their mounts on, or as they warned you to get out of their way. It was only after the race that you noticed the crowd. If you happened to be a winner, the affection of the people who'd bet on you was tepid and short-lived. After all, they'd picked the horse to win and all the jockey had had to do was to hold on and not fall off to vindicate their good judgment. If you lost, no matter how overclassed your mount might have been, the public was sure it was your fault the horse had lost. For these Monday-morning quarterbacks, the explanation was always that the jockey was completely incompetent or that he'd been paid to throw the race.

Sometimes the charges defied all logic. There are several million-dollar purses in racing today. The jockey's cut from a first-place finish in these races range from one hundred-thousand, to a hundred-and-fifty-thousand dollars. In order to have a jock pull his mount, you'd have to pay off him—or her—at least a hundred-thousand. In order for a fixer to make a killing at the betting windows, he'd have to bet three or four times that amount on another horse. Once a bet of that size went into the mutuel machines, it would lower the odds to a two-and-a-half- or five-cent profit on a dollar. There was also no hundred-percent assurance that the horse the fixer wanted to win wouldn't get beaten by an outsider, or break a leg, or have a heart attack, or suffer the million-and-one misfortunes that can befall any animal on the track. Even a guy like Marcano, who'd been able to tilt the odds in his favor, had had to borrow money from a loan shark.

I made my way to Demaret's outer office and told his secretary that I needed to see him. She told me that it was customary to make an appointment in advance, and that Mr. Demaret was very busy. I asked her to let him know I was there and she came back a moment later all smiles.

"He's on the phone right now but if you'll wait a couple of minutes, he'll be right with you," she said.

I thanked her and took a seat near the office's watercooler.

True to his word, a minute later Demaret buzzed the secretary and she directed me to go in.

Art shuffled some papers, looked at his watch, and pulled out a cigar from the inside pocket of his maroon sport jacket. "I can give you ten, maybe fifteen minutes, Eagle. What's on your mind?"

I watched him get the cigar started with an inexpensive Zippo and then he leaned back and waited for me.

"They pulled me in for the Marcano murder," I told him.

"So I heard. A cop named Fusco called to ask about you. I said you're a hothead and a jerk, but not a murderer."

"Thanks . . . I think."

"Don't thank me. They had already released you. He was just fishing to see if I had anything on Marcano."

"Do you?"

"You on a fishing expedition too, Eagle?" he asked warily.

"You might say that."

Demaret took a pull on his cigar and blew the smoke out in a series of darts. "I would have thought you'd learned something from the last time you mixed yourself in where you didn't belong."

"It seems to me that someone else mixed me in."

Demaret thought that over. "Why should I tell you anything? Maybe I'm happy to see this Marcano thing finally put to rest. The bastard made me look like the Keystone Kops."

"My guess is that you're still curious about how he got away with doping his horses. If Marcano could do it, it's only a matter of time until another trainer starts using the juice."

"Maybe I've come around to the idea that Marcano was a master trainer and he didn't juice his horses after all."

"Sure, now tell me all about the tooth fairy. Look Demaret, I'll make a deal with you. You answer my questions about Marcano, and I'll let you in on something that I found out. Who knows, maybe you can solve Marcano's murder. That might help to polish your image a bit."

He let that sink in. "I'm always willing to listen," he said cagily.

"Did you know that Marcano was in debt up to his eyeballs?"

He made a face. "Come on, Eagle. He had tax problems. Everybody knew the IRS was on his tail."

"I'm not talking about the IRS. I'm talking about one of our own neighborhood shylocks."

"Bath Beach Frankie?" His eyes narrowed.

"That's right."

"How deep was he?" He tapped the white ash of the cigar into a paper cup.

"Two hundred thousand."

Demaret gave a low whistle. "You've got my attention. What else do you know?"

"He told Frankie that he needed the money for some kind of big deal. Frankie knew what it was, but he wouldn't tell me."

Demaret nodded. "He was trying to become a partner in a breeding farm in Paris, Kentucky. He had to impress the local gentry with some heavy-duty up-front money. The deal fell through when one of the partners, a count, or a duke, balked at a low life like Marcano getting in on the action. I wondered where he got the money."

"That doesn't make sense. He could have returned the money to Frankie and been off the hook," I said.

Demaret shook his head. "No, the deal dragged on for a couple of weeks. At fifty-percent-a-week interest, he couldn't get even. He couldn't go anywhere else for the money because of the federal lien on his income."

"Who'd want him dead?"

Demaret laughed to himself. "I could make a case for a lot of people, including myself, for the way the SOB managed to elude me. You've got trainers and owners who Marcano made look equally bad." He looked up at the ceiling. "There had been some pretty intense shouting matches between Bobby Diamond and Marcano. Orlando didn't approve of the way Bobby was riding some of his nags. In fact, the rumor was that after Bobby came off suspension, Marcano was going to replace him as the stable jockey."

That caught me totally by surprise. "I thought they were good friends," I said.

"Marcano had no friends," Demaret said flatly.

"Do you know anything about Tricia dating Marcano?" I asked.

Demaret nodded. "They had quite a romance going for a while. I think she fell head over heels for Orlando and he wasn't the type of guy to stay with one woman."

Head over heels! Demaret couldn't possibly be right. It was one thing for Trish to date Marcano, but to be in love with him. . . . I took a second to conjure up a mental picture of Marcano, his gold jewelry flashing, his head thrown back laughing at the world as he put over another longshot. Trish was hanging on his arm, gazing up at the great trainer, head over heels in love. . . . I tried to make my voice sound casual.

"What do you know about her, Art? She's a mystery."

"I'm checking on her past. I found out that there were a couple of incidents at smaller racetracks that got her suspended," he told me.

I remembered the story that Bobby had told me about how when an apprentice jockey had cut her off in a race, she'd gone after him with a butcher knife.

"But Marcano put her on his horses. How come, if he'd dumped her?"

"Why not? Business is still business. You know how driven that girl is. Hey, are you okay, Eagle?"

I mustered a half-smile. "I'm just trying to figure out where she might be. She left the hospital without being discharged and nobody has seen her since."

"I haven't heard anything, but I'll let you know if I do."

"I'm not going to hold you up any longer," I said, rising. "Thank you for your help."

"Yeah sure," Demaret replied.

As the day wore on, the weather turned dark and foreboding. Snow wasn't in the forecast, which was a dead giveaway that a blizzard might hit.

People huddled in front of the thirty or so large-screen TVs the Racing Association had arranged around the grandstand, preferring to watch the action on a Sony to sitting or standing in the cold.

I watched a few races from a table in the Man O'War Room and went over the things I had learned about Trish and Marcano. Three nursed cups of coffee later found me still loaded with questions and far from any answers. I wound up leaving the track in the late afternoon just before the Eighth and Ninth Double.

■ CHAPTER 15   The Midtown Tunnel took me into the city and it was just a couple of minutes before six when I pulled into a parking lot and crossed over to Arlene Kirshbaum's office building.

A secretary seated me in a waiting room and let me know that Ms. Kirshbaum was expecting me. The area I was in, as well as the secretary's outer office, surprised me. The decor and ambiance didn't jibe with what I knew of Arlene's personality. There were dark, heavy chairs backed in an embroidered, satiny type of fabric. The chairs rested on a wine-colored carpet and the walls were mauve and garnished with ornate, flowered moldings. A large, gold-filigreed chandelier illuminated the room, casting a reflection in the only window. The window, looking down on Broadway, was framed by thick, gold drapes.

There was the staid air of "old money" permeating the surroudings. It was the kind of look that would have impressed Gus. I was sure that one of the factors that had induced him to hire Arlene to defend me was the solid and distinguished appearance of her offices.

Oddly enough, Arlene herself was nothing like the rooms. She was much closer to a Van Gogh than a Rembrandt. I had found her very down-to-earth, with the ability to roll up her sleeves and mix it up when and if she had to.

"Would you follow me please, Mr. Eagle?"

The secretary led me down a corridor and into an office where Arlene sat at a massive oak desk. We shook hands and I sat down. Her office decor was consistent with what I had seen before. The big difference was a ceiling-to-floor library filled with leatherbound law tomes, journals, and reviews that must have gone back to the turn of the century.

"Do you read any of these?"

"Not only do I read them, I find them interesting. Think there's something very wrong with me, Ken?" she asked, grinning.

I shrugged. "I don't know about that, but I will say that this place doesn't seem to be you."

"Really? What do you mean?"

"People usually stamp their own personality on their office. Aside from your degrees and honors hanging on the wall, I wouldn't know this was yours."

"You're very perceptive," she said shaking her head. "I feel like I don't really belong here myself. The office wasn't mine. I should really change it but I can't bring myself to."

"Your father's?"

"That's right. He was a very successful attorney who became a state supreme court judge. The only thing he wanted was for me to follow his footsteps, but I was a rebel. I started out as part of the Woodstock crowd, dirty feet and flowers in my hair. Then I zagged in the other direction and became a federal agent. My old crowd thought I had been working undercover and were sure I would turn them in on a pot bust. I became a lawyer about six years before Dad died. He never outwardly disapproved of anything I did. He was supportive and kind. He was very happy when I finally got into the family business, so to speak.

"This was the office I remembered as a little girl. I would play in Carol's office down the hall when my father interviewed clients. I was diapered on this desk, as a matter of fact. There's so much of him here that I find it difficult to change anything. I suppose I'll eventually have to find my own space but I never seem to have the time for that. Are your parents still alive, Ken?"

"No, they passed away a few years ago. They had a small farm in Pennsylvania. That's where I learned to ride."

The intercom buzzed and Arlene's secretary's voice came over the speaker. "Mr. Mohammad Saif is here."

"Send him in, Carol," Arlene told her.

She saw my puzzled expression.

"Even if Tricia had been able to drive with her arm in a cast, she didn't have her car at the hospital. She would have had to use a taxi or, better, hire a car. So I had my investigator copy down the names and numbers off the stickers of the different car services by the pay phone at the hospital where Trish was. There were six companies that serviced Long Island Jewish. We struck paydirt on the fourth, Acorn Car Service. My man interviewed the drivers who had worked the night before and this fellow, Saif, claimed he remembered Tricia Martin."

The door opened and Carol brought in a slight, copper-skinned man in his late twenties. He had jet-black hair, dark eyes, and a rather large nose. He seemed nervous.

"Have a seat, Mr. Saif," Kirshbaum said pleasantly. "This is Mr. Eagle."

He looked at me for a second and then turned to Arlene. "You pay me for the whole night, yes?"

"I instructed your boss, Mr. Cavanna, that we would pay Acorn to have you talk to us. We will also pay you what you would earn for an evening of driving."

"I clear one hundred dollar for one evening," he said.

"Mr. Saif, during my career as an investigator, I've had the occasion to drive a cab. On your best night you might take home sixty bucks. However, we'll pay you one hundred if you tell us all you know about a fare you picked up a couple of nights ago."

Saif raised his right hand in the air. "I swear to Almighty God that I make one hundred dollar. Honest to God, one hundred dollar. I work very hard, no breaks, drive right through. I pick up all people if they are black or brown or yellow. I take all over the city."

"All right. You'll get your money. Now tell us what you know."

Saif settled back in his chair. "When do I get money?"

"Before you leave."

"Good. I trust. Okay. That night, I get call from Cavanna, the dispatch, to pick up woman at Long Island Jewish

Hospital. The call come maybe one-thirty, two in the morning. I go there, I see little woman, pretty face with arm in cast. She have a bruise on face."

"Where did you take her?"

"In Forest Hill area."

"That's where she lives," I said.

"She go in house for maybe ten, maybe fifteen minutes. She come out . . ."

"Did she have anything with her when she came out?"

"Yes, she have a little case."

"Suitcase?"

"Yes. Little, like bag, maybe."

"Okay. Then what happened?"

"She say I take her to Brooklyn."

Arlene and I exchanged glances.

"Where in Brooklyn?" I asked him.

He reached in his pocket and pulled out a piece of folded paper. "Here is address. Cavanna give me to show you."

Arlene looked at it and handed it to me. It was the two cross-streets that intersected near Marcano's house.

"She tell me to wait and then she come back maybe fifteen, maybe twenty minute later."

"Are you sure about this?" I asked.

"I swear to God." His hand shot into the air again. "Everything I say is truth. Everything. I die now if I not tell truth."

Arlene reached into a drawer and pulled out a manila envelope. She took out five different head shots of young women and laid them out on her desk. "Are any of these the woman you picked up?"

Saif took a pair of glasses from his breast pocket and looked over the photographs. "No, she not here," he said decisively.

Arlene took out five more, different, photographs. I recognized Tricia, and so did Saif.

"Yes! Here she is. This is lady."

"Then where did you take her?" Arlene asked him.

"Back to hospital, and I go back to garage."

"Did the lady say anything to you?"

Saif shook his head. "She say nothing. Very quiet. No talking, but look like much thinking."

Arlene kept Saif for another ten minutes just to go over all the things he had said. Saif stuck to his story and if I had

91

been a member of a jury, I would have believed him completely. After assuring Saif that Carol would take care of his money, Arlene saw the driver to the door.

"I don't know what to make of all this," I told her as she slipped back behind her desk.

"Just before you got here, I got a call from the owner of Acorn Car Service, that Mr. Tony Cavanna whom Saif mentioned. It seems that Lieutenant Fusco has been making inquiries also."

"Fusco? How in the world did he find out that Tricia left the hospital earlier?"

"Perhaps the doctor that helped you . . ." she offered.

"He might have felt he was doing his civic duty. I know Fusco didn't get it from my office. I called him to find out what was going on and he had no idea that I was going to interview Saif."

"Another one of those tips, then?"

"He wouldn't say. Ken, is there anything, even the most obscure thing, that Tricia might have said to you when you spoke to her at the hospital after Marcano died?"

"You mean about where she was the night before? No, not a word. She seemed a little preoccupied but I put it down as shock over Marcano's death. The whole thing is so unlike Tricia."

"Maybe you never really knew her," Arlene said mildly.

I thought about what both Demaret and Bath Beach Frankie had told me about Tricia dating Marcano.

"There is something I have to tell you," I said.

I went through those two conversations. Arlene didn't say very much. I watched her play with a lock of hair as she listened intently.

"She never told you anything about Marcano?" she asked when I had finished.

"No. I guess you're right, I never really knew her."

I handed Arlene the address book I had taken from Tricia's home and explained to her how I learned that none of the Georgians in it had ever heard of Tricia Martin.

"She's not from Rome, Georgia," Arlene said. "We did a check on her from the track records and from some of my old sources. She was born and raised in Oran Grove, Florida. I find it strange that there isn't anybody listed in this book from her old hometown."

"Arlene, do you have any idea what's going on?"

She thought about it for a few moments. "I'm not sure. I think I know what a good district attorney would argue. Are you sure you want to know?"

I nodded.

"Ken, Tricia Martin doesn't have a spotless record. There were a couple of suspensions of her jockey license for fighting, and one suspension for menacing with a deadly weapon. That weapon happened to be a knife. She had her driver's license suspended a few years back when she was in Texas for driving while intoxicated."

"I've heard of much worse records than that."

"I'm looking at Tricia the way a Vince Fusco would. He'd say, just as Demaret did, that Marcano found someone else. This enraged Tricia. Then when one of Marcano's doped horses fell with her, almost killing her and taking her out of the race for the jockey title, she had to get even."

"I can't believe—"

"Let me finish. She might have been thinking about this for a long time. She had access to your shirt and watch when she was in your apartment, or she could have gotten at your locker in the jockey's quarters and taken your keys, made duplicates, and returned them without you being the wiser."

"You mean, all along she was just setting me up?"

"Ken, these are possibilities. She takes a car from the hospital, goes home, picks up the knife and watch, and then goes to Marcano's house. She kills him and calls you. You said yourself that you couldn't tell if the voice was a man's or a woman's."

"Saif said he took Trish back to the hospital."

"So?"

"How did my shirt with Marcano's blood wind up in my closet if she went back to the hospital?"

"It needn't have been put there the night Marcano died. Trish had the next morning after she left the hospital to herself, and if she had a key to your apartment, she just had to plant the shirt then. You were still at the track. Then she called the police and took off to parts unknown."

"You won't get me to believe that," I said, shaking my head.

"Look, Ken, you're my client. As far as I'm concerned, the one given in this murder is that you didn't do it. After that, everyone is a suspect. It may not be the best scenario in the world, but it does explain how you could have been framed. I play the hand that's dealt to me."

"What now?" I asked dejectedly.

"We try to locate Tricia Martin. I'm going to send one of my investigators to Oran Grove and see if we can find her."

"You think she went there?"

"No, I don't. It is, however, a logical place to start. There may also be people there who could shed some light on where she might be."

"Don't send anyone. I'll go."

Kirshbaum shook her head. "I don't think that's a good idea. You don't have the training and—"

"I know how to ask questions, and you yourself told me that I was perceptive."

"Ken, you shouldn't go for the same reason that doctors don't operate on family members, and lawyers don't represent themselves. You're too emotionally involved. Your involvement with Tricia is going to cloud your judgment. For all we know, your going might also be dangerous."

"I'm going," I said stubbornly.

"You're going?"

"I'm going!" I repeated.

"That's what I thought you'd say," Arlene sighed. "Take Tricia's picture and this background-check information. You're booked on an Eastern flight to Orlando. That will put you about an hour from Oran Grove. You'd better call in to my office every day, in case Fusco wants to talk to you."

"Will Fusco be a problem?"

"I'll tell him you decided to go to Disney World," she said, smiling.

■ CHAPTER 16   Oran Grove was about what you would expect of a town with a population just a shade under five hundred.

I cruised down Main Street in the rented Plymouth Fury

94

and took note of the town's businesses. There was a gas station, a diner, a pharmacy, two small grocery stores, a church, and the Oran Grove Elementary School. Citrus Avenue was situated between an interstate and a country road. I followed it down to a small lake, and eventually came to a fork. One road led back to the interstate, the other, in the direction of Titusville. I had been told that Tricia Martin's childhood home was about a quarter of the way to Titusville.

Fifteen minutes later I was standing in front of a rundown wooden frame house that wasn't actually a shack but didn't miss by much. The front yard was overgrown with weeds. A stone walkway that led to the front door was badly in need of repair.

I noticed a pickup truck parked along the side of the house, and a swing made out of an inner tube hanging from a rope attached to a tree branch. I had had something like that when I was a kid. There was no name on the door, just a brass knocker. I tapped it gently a couple of times and heard a dog bark from within.

The woman who answered might have been pretty once. Her features were attractive enough but her lank, unkempt hair and her tired demeanor soured her appearance. She could have been thirty, but she looked ten to fifteen years older.

There were no sets of locks and alarms on the door the way there are in New York, and she opened it wide. Behind her, a brood of five or six young children lay on the floor doing homework and watching television. Perhaps six children was reason enough for her to seem so prematurely old. At any rate, she wasn't old enough to be Tricia's mother.

"I'm looking for a Mister or Missus Martin. Can you tell me if they live here?"

"I'm Priscilla Martin. Who are you?"

I explained who I was and that I was interested in talking to her about Tricia.

She looked at me in an odd way. "Tricia, huh?" she said.

"You're too young to be her mother," I offered.

"Her mother was the first Mrs. Martin, Jessica. She moved out about ten years ago. I married Charlie after that. These here are our kids." She made a slight gesture indicating them with her head.

"Tricia and I were friends in New York and I was hoping I might ask you a few questions about her."

"You tellin' me you're a friend of Tricia's?"

"Yes. Perhaps she might have mentioned me."

She stared at me, searching my face. She seemed on the verge of saying something, but she held herself in check. "I'll tell you what, Mr. Eagle. When you came through Oran Grove you saw a big drugstore on Main. Mr. Alfred Stamwood is the proprietor. You tell Alfred that Priscilla sent you down to talk to Charlie. I think he'd be better'n me in answering or tellin' anything about Tricia."

"All right, but—"

"You're going to have to excuse me," she said as she closed the door behind her.

Stamwood Pharmacy was a modern store with four wide aisles, plenty of bright neons, and four uniformed, perky, high-school-aged salesgirls who seemed courteous and eager to please.

I asked the girl at the cosmetic counter if she would find Mr. Stamwood for me. She tapped a small electric buzzer three times and looked toward a door at the rear of the store. Alfred Stamwood appeared a moment later wearing a white lab coat over a shirt and tie. He was a tall, gangly fellow with a black beard who brought Abraham Lincoln to mind.

I introduced myself and told him that Priscilla had suggested that he might be able to put me in touch with Charlie Martin.

He nodded. "Sure, come along with me."

We stepped to the rear door Alfred had just emerged through. It led into a short hallway. On the right there was a unisex bathroom, and another door next to it. Stamwood pushed this door open and I was right behind him.

There were five men sitting around a card table. The one empty chair, I presumed, belonged to Stamwood. He confirmed my assumption by promptly filling it.

"Charlie, this here is Mr. Eagle from New York. He was at your place earlier and Priscilla sent him down here."

Of the five players other than Stamwood, only one was wearing a uniform. He was the sheriff of Oran Grove, and he was Charlie Martin.

He looked up at me through the dark-brown–tinted lenses

of his sunglasses. "Be right with you, son," he said in a rumble of a voice.

He chased a pair of aces until the fifth card, and then threw in his hand.

"What seems to be the problem?" he asked.

"I'm a friend of Tricia. She had an accident a few days ago and she was in the hospital. I don't want to alarm you, she wasn't badly hurt. The problem is that she left the hospital on her own and didn't let anyone know where she was going. We're worried about her and we'd like to make sure she's all right. I was wondering if she's contacted you at all, or perhaps has spoken to your first wife."

The response I got reminded me of the scene in the movies where the stranger walks into the town pub and asks the local inhabitants directions to Dracula's castle. The card game stopped abruptly and every eye in the room was on me.

"Something wrong?"

"Priscilla sent you down to see me? Didn't she say nuthin' to you?"

"No."

He nodded. "I'm going out for a while with Mr. Eagle. Deal me out," he said, rising.

We walked out a back exit to a parking lot. Charlie directed me to a white police cruiser.

"Get in, Mr. Eagle," he said, appearing to be deep in thought.

I slipped onto the cracked leather seat next to him.

Sheriff Martin stared straight ahead at the wheel. He nosed the car out of town and in a couple of minutes, we were bouncing along some dusty backroad.

I kept trying to figure why my words had caused such a reaction among the card players. Charlie Martin hadn't even looked in my direction since we'd gotten in the car.

"Where are we going?" I asked in a conversational tone.

"I'm going to take you to see Tricia," he said flatly.

"She's here?"

"Yeah."

Martin was in no mood for conversation and neither was I. I found myself holding onto the car's dashboard as he insisted on taking hairpin turns much too fast.

"Take it easy," I told him after one turn when two of the car's wheels seemed to lift off the ground. He didn't answer.

We stopped in front of a stone arch with the words SA-CRED SOULS' CEMETERY carved in its face.

"What is this?" I asked him, the annoyance creeping into my voice.

"Come on," he said, getting out of the cruiser and walking down one of the finely manicured paths. I followed him for about fifty feet, then I put my hand on his elbow. He spun around.

"What's going on, Sheriff? Why did you take me here?"

"You wanted to see Tricia. Well, there she is," he said, pointing to a sleek, gray, marble tombstone.

I read the inscription: PATRICIA MARTIN—18 YEARS OLD—GOD BLESS HER SOUL.

"Now you tell me what the hell is going on," Charlie Martin demanded.

He was sitting on a neighboring tombstone. He had taken his service revolver from its holster and it was in his hand, resting on his lap. "If this is a practical joke of some kind, it ain't funny. If this is some kind of game you're runnin', you're going to be one sorry sonofabitch."

"If this is some kind of game, it's against me . . . not you. I don't know what's going on. How long has your daughter been dead?"

"Nine years in April."

"Look, Sheriff. There's a female jockey in New York named Tricia Martin. What I told you about the hospital was the truth. What I didn't tell you was that there is also a murder investigation going on. I came down to try to find out what I could about Trish so I could find her. She may be a key to the investigation. According to the track records, she was born in Oran Grove. She listed the house you live in with your wife as her home address. If you let me reach into my pocket, I'll show you a picture of the woman."

"Let's see it," the Sheriff said.

I gave him the information Arlene had given me and he studied the black-and-white glossy of the Trish Martin I knew.

"She's not from around these parts," Martin said. "I've never seen her before."

He looked over Trish's biography. When he handed it

back to me, I noticed with no small relief that he had holstered his gun.

"There isn't any other Martin family around here?"

"Nope. Why would somebody want to pretend to be my daughter?"

"I don't know."

The two of us turned to look at the solid slab of gray stone.

"A person doesn't assume an identity unless they're running away from something," Charlie told me. "I don't like the idea of somebody using my little girl like that."

"How did Tricia die? If you don't mind my asking."

"Auto accident. A fellow in a semi, driving drunk on the wrong side of the road. My daughter's car went off the shoulder and turned over. She died instantly. I guess we can be thankful for that. The fellow who killed her got off with a couple of years. Then he got himself killed in a bar fight.

"You said something before about a murder investigation. Why don't you tell me the full story on our way back to town," Charlie suggested.

We were driving back on Main Street as I finished telling the Sheriff the full story.

He shook his head. "I don't get it. I just don't get it," he repeated.

■ CHAPTER 17

"Where are you?" Arlene wanted to know. "The phone connection isn't too clear."

"In a Holiday Inn on the outskirts of Rome, Georgia."

"You're going to talk to the people whose numbers were in Tricia's phone book. Say, what happened in Florida?"

"I found out that there is no Tricia Martin."

"Run that by me again?"

"The person we've been calling Tricia Martin is an imposter. The real Tricia Martin died about nine years ago at the age of eighteen. I showed her father our Tricia's photograph and he said he'd never laid eyes on her before."

"Are you sure?"

"If it's a ruse, the whole town's in on it. It seems the kid was everybody's favorite teenager and the story of how she got killed is one of the town's big tragedies."

"You mean our Tricia took over this kid's identity?"

"It looks that way, Arlene. She's been Tricia Martin for a long time. It coincides with when she started her riding career. I guess she applied for her jockey's license as Tricia Martin so her fingerprints wouldn't be different if she got retested. Originally, she got by using a false ID."

"Wouldn't the Racing Association do a better job of policing than that?"

"It depends. If she started in a minor league 'bull ring,' she could pay a few bucks and have the investigator certify her free and clear. Hell, in some of those places the horses are so brittle they'll take anyone who's willing to risk his life on the back of one of those nags."

"Do you have any idea who our Trish really is?" Arlene asked.

"Maybe I'll find that out today. I've got a couple of appointments. One is with the Pusey family that I spoke to over the phone from New York. The other person was just listed in the book as 'Diane.' They said they'd see me this afternoon. I intend to show them the picture I have. Maybe they can give a name to it."

"How are you getting along through all this, Ken?"

"I'm numb, but I'm still going to follow through."

Things, it turned out, were quiet in New York. No one had a clue where the person who had called herself Tricia could be. Arlene took down the number of the Holiday Inn and warned me, once again, to be careful.

■ The Puseys lived in a housing development called Happy Haven. Happy Haven was composed of identical-looking brown-and-gray townhouses, seven blocks of them, in a spoke-of-a-wheel design around a lake, a large pool, and the development's clubhouse.

I had called Mr. and Mrs. Pusey earlier in the day and told them I was the same Ken Eagle who had spoken to them from New York. I explained that I was in town investigating the disappearance of a young woman and if they could spare a few minutes of their time, it might help a great deal.

They said they would be happy to help, but they didn't think they would be able to shed any light on the Tricia Martin case. Gloria explained that when both she and Oliver had gotten off the phone with me the last time, they'd racked their brains trying to remember anyone by that name. However, they graciously agreed to see me.

Gloria Pusey turned out to be an attractive redhead in her mid-thirties. She wore a simple yellow print housedress and she answered the door with a dustrag in her hand.

Once again the door was swung wide open in response to the knock. No one asked who was there, or peeked through the door behind a latch chain. The lack of paranoia is one of the charms of the South.

"Won't you come in, Mr. Eagle," Gloria said.

I followed her into a contemporary living room. The floor was highly polished wood with a couple of tasteful throw rugs. One wall was mirrored, giving the room the illusion of being larger than it actually was. A sectional brown sofa stood near an upright piano on the wall opposite the door.

"Please excuse the appearance of the house. We've only moved in a few months ago and we're not nearly furnished. Can I get you something?"

"No, thank you."

"Please, how about a cup of coffee? I'm going to have one myself."

"Well, if it's no trouble."

"None at all." She went on talking from the kitchen. "I'm sorry Oliver isn't here. He just went out to the hardware store. When we moved in they told us that they were going to do something about the garage doors. When the garages were built they purchased a gross of locks for the doors. Well, the whole bunch of them were defective. Every so often you pull your car in and then you've got to pray that the key opens the lock so you can pull out. Management is forever promising that they are going to do something about it but they just never do. Ollie just got tired of waiting. He and a couple of the other men on the block are going to buy new locks and send the bill to the management company."

She came back into the living room and sat across from me on the couch.

"Perhaps we should wait for him," I suggested.

"He should be back any moment. What was it you wanted to know?"

I told her the story, which had by now become second nature to me. Trish Martin, a friend and fellow jockey, had suffered a concussion in a riding accident. She'd left the hospital without telling anyone where she was going and we were very concerned about her.

"Well, I sure would like to help, but . . ."

"I know, you don't know any Tricia Martin. Perhaps you'd be kind enough to take a look at the girl in this photograph."

I handed her the picture and watched her reaction. "Mister Eagle, there must be some mistake. This isn't any Tricia Martin. This is my sister—Courtney Reed," she said, surprised.

"Your sister? Are you sure?"

"Of course I'm sure. I should know my own sister!"

"What's this about Courtney?"

I hadn't heard the man walk in. Gloria's husband was a heavyset man with a stubble of beard à la Don Johnson—or else he'd forgotten to shave that morning. He came over to the sofa and extended his hand. "I'm Oliver Pusey. You must be Mr. Eagle."

"Make it Ken."

"I take it you know my sister-in-law, Courtney."

Before I could answer, Gloria grabbed my hand. "How serious was this head injury?" she asked with a great deal of concern.

"I think she's all right. We're just trying to locate her to be sure."

"How did it happen, Ken?" Oliver wanted to know.

"She was riding a race and fell off her horse."

"A race?"

Oliver and Gloria exchanged puzzled glances.

"He says Courtney's a jockey in New York, Oliver."

Oliver shook his head. "There's something wrong here. Courtney isn't a jockey, and she isn't in New York. We got a call from her about a month ago. She was leaving the States for Kenya. She's in the Peace Corps," Oliver explained.

"Kenya?" I heard myself say.

"Yes, sir," Oliver nodded.

"That's in Africa," Gloria explained, trying to be helpful.

"Could you tell me how long Courtney's been in the Peace Corps?" I asked.

Gloria wrinkled her forehead and tapped the tip of her nose. "It's got to be about five or six years by now, right, hon?"

"Six years," Oliver said. "She comes by to visit with Gloria and me when she's between assignments—last time was Christmas before last. They send her all over the States, and to some pretty exotic countries."

"Show him the postcards and letters, hon," Gloria told her husband. Oliver nodded and walked into the bedroom.

"I guess there's some kind of mix-up with those photos. Courtney's doing just fine now."

"Now?"

Gloria smiled. "Well, it ain't no secret that my sister was a hell raiser. From the very start, she was a handful. My momma and daddy took her out of an orphanage when she was six and they just couldn't do much with her. She ran off a couple of times before her thirteenth birthday, and when she was eighteen she ran off for good."

Oliver sat down next to his wife. He placed a number of postcards and letters on his lap, looked them over quickly, and then handed them to me.

The postcards were from countries in Europe, as well as from New Zealand and Australia. They featured pictures of typical tourist attractions. I checked the postmarks, and they looked genuine, as did the handwriting—it seemed definitely to be Trish's.

The letters were from major U.S. cities. I noticed that the stationery came from hotels that were situated near racetracks. I gave the writing a quick glance. There were paragraphs describing Peace Corps training, with an emphasis on taking courses in agriculture. But a Peace Corps volunteer wouldn't jaunt around all over the place. She'd stay in the country she was assigned to.

I had come to Georgia in order to tie up the loose ends of Trish's background. Instead, I was opening the door to a room filled with a lot more questions than answers.

"Why do you think she ran away?" I asked Gloria, putting the correspondence in her outstretched hand.

"There was this young fellow that came through town and Courtney started seeing him. My folks felt he was up to no good so they forbade Courtney from having anything to do with him."

"Only pushed them closer together," Oliver offered knowingly.

"That's a fact," Gloria agreed. "One day the boy was gone and Courtney with him. It kind of broke my folks' hearts, because even with her wild ways, they were both real fond of her."

I finished my coffee and thanked them for all their trouble. Not knowing what else to say, I agreed with them that there must have been some kind of mix-up. I promised that I would get back to them when I finally had the facts.

"Diane" turned out to be, as Gloria had said, a high-school classmate of Courtney Reed. She didn't really remember Courtney too well, but she did recall that Courtney could be a lot of fun. Like Gloria and Ollie, she didn't know too much about the boy Courtney had gotten involved with. He was a stranger in town, very good-looking, and she thought his name was Brian but wasn't sure.

I thanked her for her help and then drove back to the Holiday Inn.

There were several other names in the address book that Tri . . . Courtney had listed. I debated whether I would find out anything new if I got in touch with them.

When I arrived in the lobby the desk clerk called me over. "Mr. Eagle, you got a long-distance phone call from someone named Kirshbaum."

"Yes, Arlene Kirshbaum. Was there a message?"

"Only to call her back."

I dialed New York and Carol, Arlene's secretary, put me right through.

"Hi, Ken. Have you got a name for our mystery lady?"

"I've got a name, Courtney Reed, R-e-e-d. The only trouble is her brother and sister-in-law have postcards and letters that she's sent them over the last six years describing her exploits as a volunteer in the Peace Corps."

"The Peace Corps? Are you kidding? They've got to be phony. If it's the same woman."

"I'm sure it is. The letters I can explain. Trish wrote them from hotels near racetracks. I've stayed in a couple of them myself over the years, but unless Trish did some extensive overseas traveling, how was she able to send the postcards?"

"That wouldn't be a problem. There are three places on Forty-second Street I know of that will make up any kind of postmark you like, and add the foreign stamps. All you need is twenty bucks apiece. There're a few places that do it in L.A. and in a lot of other big cities. Courtney Reed, huh? I'll have a friend run a check on her. You did very well, Ken— maybe I should offer you a position with the firm."

"I'll hold you to that when I retire from the track. Now you tell me what's up. You could have waited for my news."

"I said you were perceptive. Okay, the other shoe has dropped. You're off the hook for the time being. But Miss Courtney Reed, aka Tricia Martin, isn't so lucky. Fusco has a warrant out for her."

"A warrant! Why?"

"They found the knife they're sure was used on Marcano. It was stuck in the mattress underneath the hospital bed in Tricia's—make that Courtney's—hospital room."

■ Gus picked me up at the airport and drove me to my apartment. He told me the details of how the knife had been discovered. An orderly was mopping the room and started to clean under the bed. As he pushed the mop back and forth, he heard the sound of something falling. He thought it might be part of the bed's mechanism, but when he looked underneath he saw the knife, which had been thrust into the underside of the bed's mattress. The mop head had dislodged it.

"I guess there's no doubt that it was the knife used in the Marcano murder," I said, thinking aloud.

"The police are convinced it is," Gus concurred, lighting one of his malodorous cigars.

My thoughts drifted to the good times I had spent with

Tricia/Courtney. "You know, Gus, I just can't believe that I could be such a poor judge of character."

"From what you told me on the way back from the airport, Courtney Reed has made a practice out of fooling people."

"This could still be a frame-up, Gus. Someone did it to me, they could be doing it to Courtney, too."

Gus stared at the tip of his cigar and chose his words carefully. "There's an old saying among gamblers that you don't bet on a team from your own hometown. Most of the time you wind up being carried away by emotion rather than the facts. The same thing holds true in racing. I once had five trainers tell me to bet on their own nag. Five trainers in the same race, mind you, and each swore his horse was a lead-pipe cinch. The winner turned out to be a thirty-to-one shot that took his trainer by complete surprise. The point is, Ken, that your emotional involvement with this broad is clouding your thinking. If it quacks like a duck, if it waddles like a duck, and if it swims like a duck . . . it's a duck!"

"Gus, I've been around gamblers also. There's a good percentage of them that are hunch players."

"Meaning?"

"I've got a hunch about Courtney Reed. I don't think she's a killer."

"Does that mean that you're going to pursue this?"

"I think I'll need another few days."

Gus sighed. "Suit yourself, Ken. But let's say that your theory is correct. What do you do now? You can't find the woman, you've got no hard evidence, just your hunch . . ."

"I'm not sure, but there's a big piece of the puzzle that's still missing and I think it may be the key."

"Namely?"

"The person or persons who helped Marcano dope his horses. We know that Orlando was being watched. Hell, he was under a microscope! So somebody else was juicing up his horses and it had to be someone Marcano trusted."

"You think this person was the same one who killed him?"

"I just think that whoever it was could give us a leg up on solving this thing and since Marcano had been doping his stock for a long time, it couldn't have been Courtney."

Gus thought it over. "You're not thinking it was Bobby Diamond, are you?" Gus asked, his eyes narrowing suspiciously.

"I'm not ruling him out, Gus. Demaret told me that he and Marcano were on the outs. Marcano was going to give his horses to Courtney to ride."

"Come on, Ken! That's just backstretch gossip. You know better than to listen to that stuff."

"It's just a possibility. Don't forget, Gus, he had access to my locker. He could have taken my keys."

Gus shook his head. "I've known Bobby for years. He's not the kind of person who would do anything like that. I'll tell you what I think, Ken. I think that you don't want to admit the obvious. I'm sorry, pal, but the girl made a fool out of you and tried to use you. You wouldn't be the first guy that's happened to and believe me, you won't be the last. For some reason, you don't want to accept that. You're even trying to bring Bobby into this. It just so happens that Diamond is a rival for the girl's affections. Wouldn't it tie everything into a nice neat bow for you if Bobby was Marcano's killer?"

"Come on, Gus, you know me better than that," I said weakly.

I wasn't looking for a scapegoat just to clear Trish. Or was I?

"I do know that it's time for you to get back to work. Your job is booting home winners, not running around the country searching for this girl. Leave that to the professionals, for chrissakes. That's their job. You got a leak, you call a plumber. You got a toothache, you go to a dentist. You got a—"

"Damn it, Gus! That's it!" I said excitedly.

"What's it?"

"That's what we've been doing wrong. We've been talking to people like Art Demaret about how Marcano juiced his horses. Demaret's the wrong person. You said it . . . you've got to go to a professional. If you want to find out how a race is fixed, the person to see is a fixer."

"I'm afraid to ask what that's supposed to mean," Gus groaned.

"Mark Russell."

"Mark Russell! Now I know you're crazy, for god's sake! Kenny, have you forgotten that Mark Russell almost had you killed?"

107

I hadn't forgotten. Mark Russell, also known as Marco Roselli, or simply as "The Bank," wasn't a man anyone could forget. He was the one whose money financed all the big bookie operations on the East Coast. People like Bath Beach Frankie worked only with his permission and for a large franchise fee. I had gotten mixed up with him because of a betting coup masterminded by two trainers, Milton and Austin Parrish. They had beaten Russell out of over two million dollars and I'd become their unwitting accomplice when they kidnapped my daughter, Bonnie, to ensure my cooperation.

Russell had believed my innocent role in the Parrish scheme, but that wasn't enough. He explained that the people in the street thought I was behind the coup and he would have to kill me to save face. The two million dollars was just small change compared to his reputation.

The only thing that had saved me from being killed by Russell on the spot was the fact that he was very fond of me. When he had started out as a young bookmaker, some of the old-timers had wanted to ruin him. They'd set up a "boat-race" and wagered more money than Russell could pay out. Almost every jockey in the race was in on the fix except for the jockey on a fifty-to-one shot who no one in his right mind believed could win. But I did win, and it got a grateful Mark Russell off the hook.

"At that moment, I could have married you," he had told me. "I said to myself, 'I owe Ken Eagle.'"

He'd paid me back by allowing me two whole days to expose the Parrish brothers. If I hadn't been able to succeed, I had no doubt that Mark Russell would have been true to his word and I would have ended up wearing cement underwear.

"Hey Kenny, when your parents took you to the zoo, did you beg them to lock you up in the tiger cage?"

"Gus, it makes sense," I reasoned. "No one has been able to figure out how Marcano did it. If anyone would know, it would be Russell."

"Okay, okay. Let's say that Russell does know. What the hell gives you the idea that he's going to tell you? Why should he? You know, Ken, just because he didn't kill you doesn't make him your bosom buddy."

"It's worth a try," I insisted. "What do I have to lose?"

"Oh, nothing much. Just your life . . ."

■ CHAPTER 18 Getting in touch with Mark Russell wasn't as easy as looking him up in the phone book. Everything had to go through channels.

I relayed my interest to Bath Beach Frankie, who promised he would pass it along. He warned me that the request for an appointment made its way up the chain of command and anywhere along that chain, someone might turn thumbsdown and I would be out in the cold. Frankie advised me to stay by my phone.

At 5:45 the phone rang. The voice on the other end told me that Mr. Russell would see me at a place called Pasta Presto on Second Avenue. I was to be there at 6:15 sharp.

I grabbed a cab and made it with at least twelve seconds to spare.

Mark Russell was sitting by himself in a small booth. Even though I had met him before, I was still surprised by his youth. He didn't look older than thirty and yet, because of his reputation, it seemed that he had been around forever.

He looked up and nodded to me. I walked over and slid into the booth opposite him.

"I remembered that you don't drink. I think I read it somewhere. Am I right?" he asked.

"I don't care for the taste, I can't afford the calories, and there was a time in my life that I had a problem with the stuff."

"I admire a man who knows his limitations. I ordered you a diet soda."

"Thanks."

Russell was one of those people who had what they call in show business, *"presence."* Although in no way physically imposing, he had a kind of assurance in how he spoke and in the way he carried himself that even if you didn't know him, would draw your eye. He was about five-ten, with short, black curly hair. His chin and nose could have been carved in granite, taken directly off the old Roman coins depicting the Caesars. Only his soft, brown eyes contrasted the otherwise hard, masculine face. He was wearing tight-fitting jeans and a white cableknit fisherman's sweater.

He handed me the menu. "You're still riding, aren't you, Ken?"

"I've taken a few days off. I should be back in the irons in a day or so."

If he had heard about my involvement in the Marcano murder, he wasn't letting on. He looked over the menu.

"The reason I ask is that everything on this menu might be too fattening for you. I got an idea. I'll have them bring you a bowl of spaghetti without any butter or oil. You put a little bit of marinara on that and you'll enjoy it. It's got very little fat, lots of carbohydrates, and it's low in calories."

"That sounds great," I told him.

"Just don't be jealous when you see what's on my plate," he kidded.

A waiter appeared out of nowhere and took Mark's order. Over his shoulder I could see the restaurant's manager watching very carefully, hoping to please—or at the very least, not displease—Mr. Russell.

"So what's on your mind, Ken? You can speak freely to me."

I gave him a bare-bones breakdown of the Marcano case. He listened attentively, asking appropriate questions and nodding in all the right places.

"So, both you and now your lady friend have been implicated in this thing?"

I nodded.

"Now that I see the whole picture, tell me what you want of me?"

"You have to be aware that Marcano's horses were being juiced," I said to him.

He shrugged. "I heard things. I understand he had something that turned milk horses into champions. It never really affected my business so I didn't pay much attention to it. I mean, a lot of people were winning by backing Marcano's ponies, but the odds went down so low it didn't really matter. I have a personal aversion to drugging animals. I don't think it's good for the game. It just creates doubt as to the honesty of the sport and in the long run, it's bad for the bookie trade."

"So you never really checked into it?"

"There were other things that took precedence. I guess in retrospect, I let it slide."

"I was hoping you'd help me find out how he did it."

Russell smiled. "You're thinking of becoming a trainer?"

"No. The way I see it, if I can find out who was involved with Marcano, I may get to his real killer."

Russell thought it over. "Okay, and what do I get out of it?"

"Well, you said yourself it was bad for business."

"Yeah, but Marcano and his potion are history now."

"Somebody else could use the stuff."

"I'll worry about it then."

I took a couple of bites of spaghetti and tried to come up with some inducement to get Russell to help me. Nothing came to mind.

"You see, Ken, there's something you've got to understand. Everything is a commodity. I have to admit that I have a soft spot for you, and I sympathize with your trying to clear this Courtney woman. I mean, you wouldn't believe it, but I'm really a hopeless romantic. The thing is, I got to get something out of this if I help you."

"What can I offer you?"

Russell speared a piece of broccoli with his fork. "It can be open-ended. Let's just say that you owe me one," Mark said with a disarming smile.

I thought of Gus's image of stepping into the tiger cage. There would be a race that Mark would want to win and I could visualize him asking me to pull my horse, or take a quick fall off my mount. It was that or maybe some inside information, or God knows what . . .

"I'd feel more comfortable if things were spelled out," I told him.

"Ken, don't you trust me?" He looked annoyed.

"I'm learning from you, Mark. Business is business, and I want to be sure I can meet my obligations."

He smiled. "You don't trust me, but I like the diplomatic way you said it. Look, I've got an idea. I've got a yearling in Florida. The horse's name is Ginny's Little Guy. Virginia is my girlfriend and she always wanted a horse, so I got her one. Remember what I told you about me being romantic? Well,

111

I'm thinking I want to race the sucker at Saratoga in the summer. You know, in those classy two-year-old allowance races. What I want from you is a firm commitment that you'll ride him any time I ask you to."

"To win?"

"Of course to win! What do you think I'm going to do, ask you to stiff my girl's horse? That four-legged Lamborghini already set me back a million-six. I'd like to try and win some of it back."

I would have to okay the arrangement with Gus and Joe Herrera, but I knew that would be no problem.

"You've got a deal, Mr. Russell."

"Good!"

He extended his hand and we shook on it. "Now you finish your meal and have a cup of coffee. When you walk out of here there'll be a chauffeured limo waiting. He'll take you to the wizard. I hope you find out what you want, but don't forget, even if you don't, we have a deal. Now I'm off to Lincoln Center for a dose of culture. You take care of yourself," he said as he got up to go.

The limousine was there as Mark Russell had promised. The driver opened the door for me and told me that Mr. Russell had given him directions on his car phone about where to take me. He took a black hood out of his pocket.

"When we get a few miles from where we're going, I'm going to have to ask you to put this hood on. It's a security precaution," he explained.

I told him it would be okay. We headed out of the city and into Jersey through the tunnel, and then south. We were traveling in the direction of Atlantic City. After about an hour, the driver pulled off at a roadside diner.

"Time to put on your outfit," he said, handing me the hood. "Do me a favor and don't take it off until I tell you to. Otherwise, you might really complicate things," he said ominously.

"The last thing I want to do is complicate things," I said. I placed the hood over my head. "How long will I have to wear this thing?"

"It won't be long now."

We must have driven another fifteen or twenty minutes. Whether it was done to confuse me, or out of necessity, it seemed to me as if we were doing a lot of driving around in circles. Then the feel of the road changed from smooth highway to a more choppy and uneven surface, and finally to a long stretch of gravel. We stopped and I heard the door open beside me. I felt the chauffeur's hand slip under my shoulder and he helped me out of the car.

"When you hear the door close behind you, you can take it off. There'll be somebody waiting for you."

I heard a door opening and immediately felt the change of temperature as I was gently pushed forward. I waited for the door to close and then took off the hood.

I wasn't prepared for what I saw. Standing directly in front of me was a black female midget. I took her to be about fifty, but her silver-gray hair and thick, black glasses might have been deceptive.

"What are you staring at? You've seen little people before. You're not exactly Kareem Abdul Jabbar yourself," she said good-naturedly. "I'm the wizard Mark Russell told you about. You can call me Sarah. Follow me please and don't touch anything!"

The building was large and modern. We walked along a neon-lit hallway past a number of laboratories. A skeleton crew was working at this late hour, made up mostly of Asians. They paid little attention to Sarah and me as they stirred beakers or punched numbers into their computers. Someone had invested a lot of money in this place. The various labs looked clean and new and the equipment seemed to be state of the art.

Sarah's office turned out to be a very simple room with a gray Formica desk and a couple of modern leather chairs. There were two paintings, one a seascape and the other a still life featuring a bowl of fruit. There was nothing else around that could give me a clue as to where we were. The fact that there were no windows anywhere didn't help matters in that regard either.

"This belongs to Mark Russell?"

"Just a small nook in the vast Mark Russell empire," Sarah said.

"Yeah, his narcotics empire," I said, shaking my head.

She looked at me as if she was trying to understand what I meant. Then she threw her head back and laughed. "No . . .

no, no, no. We're not." She laughed again. "You think we make illegal drugs here like heroin and cocaine? Oh, that's funny. Do you have this picture of us taking cocaine and mixing it with baking soda to get crack, and then . . . Oh, that's too much!"

"I guess I'm wrong."

"Very much so. Not that I have a problem with making narcotics. I am a genius, you know, so the frivolousness of the world's morals and laws don't concern me. It's just that that kind of business is just so much fluff. It isn't worth our time. Oh, my goodness, between securing the raw materials, and manufacturing and setting up a distribution network, and . . ."

"Then why all the secrecy? Why did I need to wear this?" I pulled the hood from my pocket.

"That was for my protection. I used to work for the government but we had a falling out. I wanted to leave their employment and they said I couldn't. We'd rather not make it easy for them to find me," she explained.

"If this isn't a narcotics factory, then what is it?"

"We make products that no one will ever see. That's where the real money is."

"Weapons?"

"My goodness, Mr. Eagle, you have a very nefarious mind. No, not weapons, we make consumer goods that are so good they can't be distributed to the consumer. I see you're all confused. You wear shoes, don't you, Mr. Eagle? Most of the people who live on this planet wear shoes. After you wear shoes for some time, the heels wear down and the soles get thinner. In fact, if you wear the shoe long enough, you'll form a hole around the general area under the ball of your big toe. Now let's say for argument's sake that there was a polymer spray that you could apply to the soles and heels of your shoes. This chemical would bind the atoms of the leather so that they would be impervious to wear. That would mean that one pair of shoes would last a person a lifetime."

"Does something like that exist?"

"If it did, you wouldn't know about it. You see, the manufacturing of shoes and related businesses such as designing, tanning, advertising, selling—oh, perhaps ten or twelve related industries—would be devastated if shoes didn't have

114

built-in obsolescence. It is much better for them if this new discovery never sees the light of day. So they scrape together upward of a billion dollars and deposit it in a Russell Swiss bank account and bury the miracle patent deep in the corporate vaults. The same thing would hold true for the rubber industry, you could have tires that never wear out. Then there's razor blades that never get dull, batteries that could last for decades instead of weeks . . . the technology is there. It would, of course, create economic chaos and no one wants that, least of all Mr. Russell. He doesn't have to worry about getting a product to market and distributing it and all the other headaches, including having Uncle Sam as his partner. The wizard just mixes her chemicals, comes up with the magic elixir, and we show it to representatives of the targeted industry. The formula is paid for and locked away and we move on to our next challenge."

"Is that what you're in it for? The challenge?"

"You're very curious, aren't you? It's the trait of a scientist."

"I'm a jockey."

"Oh my goodness, are you? When I was a girl, at least a million people looked at my height and told me that I should be a jockey." She giggled.

"But no, I enjoy the challenge, and you're right in assuming it's not the money. I could make all the money I ever wanted in an instant. The reason is much more personal." She stared into my eyes. "Do you really want to know?"

"Yes."

"Quite frankly, there are certain objects of art that appeal to me. I enjoy acquiring these things and sometimes, unfortunately, they belong to someone else. Mr. Russell, through his contacts and power, is able to acquire what I need. He is like me in the fact that he has no moral restraints. I think we'd best leave it at that," she said, smiling.

"Now let's get back to you. What brings you to the wizard?"

It was hard to think of this seemingly sweet little woman as an art thief, but that wasn't what I was there for. I told her about Marcano—how he had turned the racing world inside out by claiming a poor-to-mediocre horse from another trainer and then making that same horse into a world beater.

"I could name at least fifteen or twenty different sub-stances that could do that," she said evenly.

"What about escaping detection?"

I told her of the elaborate post- and pretest drug screening procedures that the track had contracted Cornell University to perform.

"A good chemist can get around that. You'd have to change some molecules on a proportional basis and you might have to add a substance or two as a screen."

"There's one other thing. The horses are mild before the race and then come out like tigers once the starting gate is opened," I added.

"Then the drug is administered within minutes of the start," she said matter-of-factly.

I shook my head. "The horses are being watched. They've made videotapes of every step the horse takes outside the paddock."

"The drug I'm thinking of requires a hypodermic needle, say, about seven inches long."

"No. No way. There's no way they could stick a horse with something like that in full view of twenty thousand peo-ple and two dozen racing officials."

Sarah put her hands on her hips. "Well, then there's no drug that can be used that can match the criteria you've set up for me."

"Are you sure? What about something new?"

"Mr. Eagle, don't insult me! If I say there's nothing, there's nothing. Are you sure you've given me all the facts?"

"As much as I know."

"Let's see . . ." Sarah looked up at the ceiling and tapped her fingers on the edge of the desk. "We've got to worry about detection . . . and the drug is fast-acting . . . and it has no residual because whoever buys it back from Marcano gets a broken-down animal . . . and it's administered without a hypo. . . . No, I'll stick by my statement. There's no single drug that can meet all those specifications."

I sighed deeply. "I guess that's it then."

Wherever Marcano was, he had to be laughing up his sleeve.

Sarah ignored my words as well as my look of disappoint-ment. She began pacing.

"Synergism!" she said, looking up at me and nodding. She had a slight smile on her face.

"Beg your pardon?"

"Synergism," she said again, expecting me to know what she was talking about. She noticed my blank look and decided to explain. "Synergism is when the action of two discrete agencies in cooperate action produce a total effect that is greater than the sum of the effects taken independently."

"Which means . . ." I prodded.

"Two and two equal eight."

I stared at her dumbly.

"Mr. Eagle, you take an antihistamine and it makes you drowsy, perhaps a level-two measure of drowsiness. Had you taken a shot of whiskey instead of the antihistamine perhaps it, too, would have given you a level-two measurement of drowsiness. If, however, you had taken the two substances together, expecting to boost your level of tiredness to a four, you might be surprised to find that the level has been raised by the interaction of the two substances to a level eight or ten. That's a synergistic response. When I said that there was no single chemical that could breach the criteria you specified, that didn't mean there couldn't be combinations of chemicals that could do the trick. . . . Let me see, let me see." She began pacing again. She stared at the same spot in the ceiling. Finally, she nodded. "Yes! I see how it was done. Very elementary, and yet very clever. The drug they used is a man-made synthetic for heroin called fentanyl. It could be made many times more powerful than heroin. We don't see much of it here in the East, but it's a favorite of the California crowd. Horses' systems react very differently to heroinlike compounds. People get tired and slow down, but it makes horses think they're prancing young colts. That's what they slip the horse just before the race."

"That wouldn't require a large needle?"

"Something long enough to puncture horsehide would be detectable, but here's the good part. Sometimes up to three weeks before the race, the horse is injected with corrasalin. That's a long-acting drug that can stay in the horse's system for up to a month. Corrasalin is indistinguishable from the horse's own adrenalin. It won't show up on any test. By itself, it won't do a thing for the horse's performance, but when it gets combined with fentanyl, you've got rocket fuel!"

"But wouldn't that show up?"

"Yes, but you'd have to test right after it was administered. After the race would be too late. You see, the fentanyl gets right into the bloodstream and stimulates the heart and in turn expands the surface area of the lungs. During the race the drug is expelled through kidney sweat and breathing vapor. There'd be nothing in the urine, saliva, or blood."

"But you said that the drug was given just before the race."

"The fentanyl is. It doesn't matter when the horse gets corrasalin as long as it's within a month. Somebody could inject the horse or even incorporate corrasalin in its feed."

"I still can't see how they could give the fentanyl in full public view."

"That's no problem. With corrasalin in the horse's system, a scratch of fentanyl would react synergistically. They could use a tack needle. You've never seen one? I'll show you what they look like."

She pressed a button on the phone. "Lee, get hold of some fentanyl and prepare it for me in a tack needle, and give Jefferson two cc's of corrasalin."

She released the button. "Fentanyl is a highly concentrated substance. Even so, for an animal weighing nearly a ton, you would need more than could be concealed easily. With corrasalin as a 'booster,' however, it can be hidden in a tack needle."

Less than twenty seconds later, there was a knock at the door. A young man walked in, half-bowed to Sarah, and handed her a cork. Then he walked out, bowing slightly again.

"Move your chair closer," she said to me. "We keep it in a cork to prevent sticking ourselves accidentally. Here it looks like an ordinary thumbtack, right?"

She pulled it away from the cork and reached into her desk drawer. She had a magnifying glass in her hand. She handed me the glass. "Look closely. You see what looks like a thumbtack. The top is flesh-colored, a tannish pink. That's to match the color of your palm. The head is coated with an adhesive so it can stick to your palm with the needle pointed out. With the glass you can see the pin part. Actually, it's a hollow, very thin needle made of a special material that combines the qualities of plastic and wax. The material itself is transparent. The amber color you see is the small dose of fentanyl. Now, if you were a CIA agent, you'd go over to your victim with the tack needle in place on your palm and slap him heartily on the back. A split second later your victim would be out cold or dead, depending on what drug was being administered. The needle part breaks right off in the victim's skin where it's designed to melt like wax at a temperature of ninety-eight degrees. That happens immediately and the dose gets right into the bloodstream."

"Are you saying that all a jockey has to do is pat his horse on the neck or on the rump with this thing?"

"That's all."

There wasn't a jockey in the world who didn't pat his mount gently to reassure it, or to encourage it. It was the most natural action and impossible to pick up. The drug could be administered with complete impunity.

"You implied these needles are being used by the CIA. Could a civilian get his hands on them?" I asked her.

"They don't have them at Sears, but if you want them, they can be purchased. Again . . . in California. Now, I'll show you the effects. You can follow me," she said leading the way into the hall. She held the fentanyl between her thumb and index finger.

"Just where are we going?"

"Down the hall and around that bend." She nodded ahead of us.

We passed several more doors, all of them closed, until we finally came to the area Sarah'd been looking for. These doors were wooden and painted with a shiny white lacquer. The words BIOLOGICAL SPECIMENS were stenciled in neat black letters.

Sarah opened the doors and it was as if we had entered a large pet shop. There were at least fifty different-sized cages, all holding species of animals, some two and three to a cage. There were dogs, cats, snakes, guinea pigs, mice, rats, chickens, and some exotic-looking creatures I couldn't place. The sounds, but more strikingly the smell, brought back my boyhood days on the farm.

We stopped in front of a large cage about six-by-four-by-four feet. A mid-sized German shepherd barked once, sheepishly, as if he understood it was expected but his heart wasn't really in it. He brought his head close to the bars to try to sniff us.

"No treats today, Jefferson."

The mention of the name drew my attention. She had said something before about giving Jefferson corrasalin.

"Are you thinking of injecting the dog?" I asked her.

"Of course. How else can we check the hypothesis? Jefferson weighs roughly one twentieth of an average horse. I've adjusted his dose of corrasalin accordingly. We can give him the fentanyl and then measure his motor responses on the treadmill."

"Is it really necessary?" The dog was licking my hand. I remembered the wild eyes and flaring nostrils of Marcano's doped horses. They had looked panicked, frightened out of their skins. I didn't want to see that transformation in Jefferson. "Can it be dangerous?"

"There's always some danger in the unknown, but until we carry out the experiment, all we have is a theory."

"I'll take your word for it," I told her. "Let's leave it theoretical."

Jefferson seemed to appreciate my concern. I got two fingers through the bars and patted the top of the dog's head.

"As you wish" she said, her tone implying she thought I was being very silly. I watched her place the cork she had taken from her pocket on the business end of the tack needle.

"Can I take that with me?" I asked. "It may turn out to be important evidence."

She thought about it. "I have no objections, but you would be well advised to forget where you got it."

I nodded my thanks and gingerly took the needle from her.

"You don't have to treat it so daintily. As long as the cork is on the needle, you can keep it right in your pocket. Remember, fentanyl is a heroin derivative. In animals it sends them up, but if you were to get stuck, you'd react the way humans do to heroin."

"You mean nod out?"

"Well, it would be more than a 'nod,' but it wouldn't be lethal."

I still treated the fentanyl with respect. "I appreciate your help," I told Sarah.

"No need to thank me. If I know Mark Russell, he extracted a heavy price for my services."

"He did, and it was well worth it. Quite frankly, Sarah, you amaze me. I never expected that you would be able to tell me so quickly what I wanted to know. I'm tremendously impressed."

"Well, we all do what we can. You ride horses, and I solve the riddles of the universe." She smiled.

"I'm sure you do."

"At any rate, it was nice meeting you and you did supply me with a nice diversion. I'm to take you back to the outer door now. Get your hood ready," she cautioned.

■ CHAPTER  Chester, my doorman, was impressed to see me stepping out of the limo. I had to explain to him that I hadn't hit the lottery; and no, I wasn't turning Hollywood on him.

He told me that the building management company had been around to change the cylinders of my lock and he handed me two shiny new keys for my door.

I made my way upstairs, convinced that for some reason the keys wouldn't work; I was pleasantly surprised when they did with just a minimum of sticking.

Gus had left me a message (sometimes we went through days of playing "telephone tag" with both of us leaving messages on our respective machines). From the sound of his voice, this seemed to be important.

"Ken, Arlene Kirshbaum was trying to get you but she didn't want to leave a message. She called me and I told her I'd get in touch with you. I'm afraid there's some bad news about Courtney Reed. Don't get nervous, she's all right. I mean, I guess she's all right since no one has seen her since she took off from Long Island Jewish. The bad news is about her past. It seems that when Arlene ran it down, she found out that Courtney and an accomplice were wanted for an armed robbery that resulted in a murder about ten years ago. That's all Arlene was able to come up with for the moment. She said she'd tell you whatever else her people found out as soon as she gets more information. Look, Ken, I'm awful sorry. I didn't . . ." There was a brief pause. "I think you know that I really didn't want to burst your bubble like this. I'll be home late tonight if you want to talk. I hope everything went okay with our friend, the tiger." Another pause. "Really, Ken. If you need me, call."

I stared at the machine for a good two minutes and tried to sort out my feelings. Tricia Martin, or Courtney Reed, or whatever her name was had taken me for a ride. I still found it hard to believe and couldn't fully accept what Gus had told me. The woman who had been in my arms, whom I had fallen in love with, was an armed robber and involved in a murder?

I could see clearly now what Arlene had meant about me not getting too close to the case. Gus's admonition about not betting on home teams was also buzzing around in my head.

I saw now that what I had been really trying to do the last few days was to find another suspect besides Courtney, instead of trying to find the truth. I had been ready to pin the whole thing on Bob Diamond. That made me a hell of a lot worse than Detective Vince Fusco had been with me. At least Fusco had circumstantial evidence. Okay, maybe it *was* conceivable that Bobby was in on Marcano's horse-doping scheme. I wasn't about to admit I was completely off base. From what Sarah had told me, he was the most likely to have been using the tack needle.

And he'd had a lot to gain. Not only had he made money at the betting windows, but he'd also achieved prominence as a leading jockey. Still, that was a quite a leap to him actually murdering Marcano. I had known Bobby Diamond for years and here I was, ready to throw him to the wolves.

Courtney Reed I'd known a matter of months. She had lied about her identity, she'd been close-mouthed about her past, she'd neglected to tell me about her affair with Marcano—and this was the woman I was so willing to defend?

"You should have your head examined, Eagle," I said out loud in disgust.

I got up and walked to the kitchen. The disbelief soon gave way to anger. I picked an apple out of the refrigerator and devoured it along with a handful of vitamin pills.

How long had she been planning this? The whole time she was with me, was she thinking of ways to frame me for Marcano's murder? What a lovesick puppy I'd turned out to be.

I trekked back to the living room and switched on the TV. For five minutes I watched that new actor playing Sherlock Holmes on public television. I found I couldn't get into the show. For me, Basil Rathbone was Sherlock Holmes and anything else was sacrilege. I turned the TV off and paced around the house for a while, then I filled up the bathtub but decided I didn't have the patience to sit in the tub. I was as jumpy as a turkey during Thanksgiving week. It took a conscious effort, but I finally managed to sit myself down and try to relax.

I wanted to confront Courtney. I wanted to tell her what I thought of her. I wanted to ask her how she could repay my feelings with such cold-hearted deceit.

I took out her address book and looked it over again. There had to be someone here who knew where she was hiding. The people in the book were all links to her past. By keeping their numbers, she was keeping intact the threads of her life. Tomorrow I would go through the book again. Somebody had to have some idea where the woman might be.

I noticed that on the inside cover of the black leather book, Courtney had written: J. Phillip, Sullivan County, R.E. Brokers. It started me thinking.

I grabbed the phone and got the area code for Sullivan County and called information. I asked about a listing for J. Phillip.

"No, I don't have the address."

The operator informed me that it was an unlisted number.

I asked about a business called Sullivan County Real Estate Brokers.

"That's on Field Street. Please hold for the number."

I copied it down and tried it. I knew it was way past business hours but sometimes you could catch someone working late in a real-estate office. I let it ring ten times, and then I gave up.

Certain things were coming back to me. We had once dis-

123

cussed the relative merits of living in a warm climate or a cold one. Courtney liked the cold. One of the things she'd liked best about the house she had rented in Queens was the fireplace.

"Nothing beats sitting by a roaring fire while a snowstorm howls around outside," she had said.

We had laughed at how she'd been raised in the South and liked the cold, whereas I had come from frigid Pennsylvania and loved the hot weather. She had told me that if she ever had some time to herself, she was going to rent a cabin "up North."

If you were going to get lost, Sullivan County was as good a place as any. Maybe it was just the place that would have a cabin and a fireplace.

■ The morning found me in no less black a mood, but at least I had some hope of finding Courtney.

I waited until nine o'clock to call the Sullivan County Real Estate people but no one was in the office yet. It was hard to think of people not starting work until after nine. On the racetrack, half your day was over by nine A.M.

I was about to try the number again when the phone rang. It was Arlene Kirshbaum.

"I guess Gus got the message to you?"

"Yes. I feel like I've been taken."

"Well, if it makes you feel any better, it's obvious you weren't the only one. I'm sorry I don't have very much more for you. I asked a friend of mine in the Georgia area to circulate the name Courtney Reed and although he got the hard facts, for the moment they're kind of sketchy."

I told Arlene about the lead I had developed. She listened as I told her what I'd found on the inside cover of Courtney's phone book. I didn't give her J. Phillip's name.

"You think she rented a place, or bought a place, from the person in the book?"

"That's my hope," I told her.

"You're very carefully not mentioning any of the particulars. What's the person's name and what's the name of the real-estate outfit?"

"I'm going to keep that to myself. I need to follow this up."

Arlene didn't sound happy about it. "Remember what I told you, Ken, the first time we met in Fusco's office? I said you were paying good money for my advice and you'd do well to take it. It turned out you didn't know very much about Courtney Reed. What you know now you wouldn't want to write home to mother about. She's wanted for armed robbery and she's implicated in some way in two murders. That's a pretty somber chain of events, especially for a young woman who hasn't seen her thirtieth birthday yet."

"You're telling me it could be dangerous."

"I'm telling you that you might be killed!"

Arlene's words had a chilling effect on me. I'd never considered that I could be in danger from Courtney. The thought of this woman actually causing me physical harm was just too farfetched to even pop into my head. But then again, perhaps Marcano had felt the same way.

"You might be right, Arlene. Look, I don't even know if this lead is going to pan out, but if it does . . . I'll be careful."

"You better be *very* careful. Gus is very fond of you, and I'm very fond of Gus. You wouldn't want to do anything to nip a romance in the bud, would you?"

I smiled. No wonder my agent had been so closed-mouthed about the latest development in his love life. Arlene Kirshbaum certainly broke the mold of Gus's Blonde-of-the-Week Club. I heartily approved.

"Well, if you put it that way, I'll take every precaution."

"I'd rather you took a gun. Do you have one?"

"No."

"Okay, at least let me have someone tail you until—"

"No tail, Arlene. I mean it!"

"Don't bite my head off. I've got to leave the office now. Whatever goes down, I want a phone call from you."

"Yes, Mommy," I kidded.

"Ken, nobody likes a wiseass," she said, but jokingly.

■ I tried the real-estate office again and still there was no answer. What was wrong with those people upstate? Didn't they know the old saw about the early bird?

125

Out of sheer frustration I called Sullivan County information and asked the operator to check on a listing for a Tricia Martin. When that didn't pan out, I gave her Courtney Reed. Then in rapid succession I tried Tricia Reed, Courtney Martin, Martin Reed, T. Reed, T. Martin, C. Reed, C. Martin . . . I totally crapped out but at least I had killed another twelve minutes.

I tried Sullivan County Real Estate again. I gave it my customary ten rings and I was in the process of replacing the phone in the cradle when I thought I heard a voice on the other end.

"Hello?" I said.

"Sullivan County Real Estate, how can I help you?"

From her tone, she was a trifle annoyed at having had to repeat herself.

I had my story all set. After all, I had spent a restless night practicing.

"I'd like to talk to Mr. Phillip," I said, suddenly realizing that the name sounded more like a beautician's than a real-estate agent's. *Mr. Phillip, formerly of La Chérie, will be here starting Monday for cuts and blows,* was what came to mind.

"We don't have a Mr. Phillip," the girl said.

That dashed my hopes.

"No J. Phillip?"

"Well, we do have a Jean Phillips," she told me.

You had to admire the mental agility of the receptionist to make that farflung connection.

"Yes, that's who I mean. Jean Phillips. Is she in?"

"Who may I say is calling?"

"She doesn't know me. My name is Mike Joseph and I'm with the bank."

A moment later a woman got on the phone. She sounded older, very professional. "Jean Phillips here. How may I help you, Mr.—"

"Joseph. Mike Joseph. Please call me Mike."

"All right, Mike. You're with the bank?"

"Yes, and we've had a young woman come in to apply for a loan."

"Excuse me. What bank did you say you were with?" Jean asked me.

How stupid of me not to anticipate that. Jean would know every bank in the area.

"Hello, Mr. Joseph, are you there?"

I took a shot. "Fidelity."

"Fidelity?" She sounded puzzled.

I'd blown it.

"Oh, you mean Statewide Fidelity. We just call it State-wide."

I was back in business.

"You say someone came in for a loan? Did they give us as a reference?"

"Well, the young woman mentioned that she had just done some business with you folks. Let me see, what did I do with that application. We just need to verify her address. I *know* I had that application. I was away for a week and when I came back my desk was a mess."

Jean laughed. "Believe me, I can relate to that. I leave this place for one moment and it takes me a week to get my bearings. Do you remember her name? Maybe I can help you out."

"Y'know, I had it here right in front of me. She was a pretty young girl in her late twenties . . . brown hair. She came in and filled out the application sometime last week."

"Well, we see so many people . . ."

"She had a cast on her right arm."

"Oh, you mean Karen North. Yes, the girl who was in that skiing accident," Jean said.

"That's it. Karen North. She said she'd rented a place from you people."

"Uh-huh. The Eaton house, over on Califon and Joy Road."

"Right!" I wrote it down.

"She's a lovely girl. She's waiting for her husband to come back from overseas. He's a career serviceman."

"Yes, that's the information she gave us. Thanks for your help," I told her.

"That's okay. If you need anything else, just call or drop us a note. And say hello to Dotty, the teller, for me."

"I sure will," I said. I thanked her again and hung up.

■ I wondered how Courtney was able to rent a place so easily without identification. The one thing I'd have to come to grips with was that she was an accomplished liar. I could envision her coming up with the abandoned newlywed story. Her husband had been called away to an outpost overseas and she was all alone, the victim of a skiing accident that had left her almost incapacitated.

Maybe all her identification was in her luggage and that was on the way from Aspen where she'd had the accident . . . or maybe I was making things more complicated than necessary. She'd shown up with a bagful of cash and that alone had been enough to answer any questions or doubts anyone may have had.

I had a map of New York State in my car's glove compartment and I pulled it out and looked it over. Naturally, I couldn't find Califon or Joy Roads on the map. They were local roads, and in the flush of finding Courtney I hadn't even asked what town they were near.

I wasn't going to call Jean Phillips again. That could have made her suspicious and she might have decided to warn her client.

I drove to a pay phone and got the upstate number for Statewide Fidelity Trust. A man answered and I asked for Dorothy, the name of the teller Jean Phillips had mentioned.

"Dorothy Mercer here," she said.

"Hi, Dorothy. This is Mr. Green."

"Yes," she said slowly, "do I know you?"

"Oh, maybe not. Whenever I go to the bank you always wait on me."

"Well, I'm sure I'd know you by sight. How are you today?"

"Fine. I'm calling because when I was waiting on line the man in front of me dropped a letter. I want to return it to him but the address is incomplete."

"What's the name?"

"It says Mr. Eaton, and the address is Califon and Joy Roads."

"I don't know any Eaton. Califon and Joy Roads . . . that's in Monroe. I'm surprised he does his banking here, we have a branch on Pine Lane."

"Okay, I'll send it out. Thank you."

I looked over the map again. Monroe was easy enough. It was a scoot up the thruway. Without traffic, it would take about two hours. I drove over to the East River Drive and followed the signs north . . . north to Karen North.

■ It was a cold gray day with the colors of the clouds matching the shades of the slabs of rock that bordered either side of the road. What was I going to do when I finally saw Tricia/Courtney/Karen? I felt like throttling her but I knew I wouldn't. I suppose I needed to see her to vent my anger. I wanted her to know what I thought of her as a human being.

Okay, Eagle . . . then what? Are you going to haul her off to jail? Are you going to call Fusco and have him *haul her off to jail?*

Maybe there was some explanation that would explain her actions. . . . *Cut it out, Eagle! There you go again, trying to alibi for her. This is the girl who set you up for a long fall. She deserves nothing but contempt.*

About a mile from Monroe proper, I stopped to ask for directions. Joy Road was a two-laned highway that I took for four miles. Califon was an unpaved road that intersected at a fork with another back road called Alameda.

I pulled off on the shoulder and looked around. A red aluminum mailbox was visible about twenty feet from where I had stopped. I walked toward it, marveling at how quiet the country was. The roads had been cut through a forest that seemed dark and mysterious. It seemed even more so now because of the threatening sky.

The name on the mailbox read EATON.

There was a footpath behind it and I followed it about forty feet to a clearing. I could see a small, wooden house, little more than a cabin actually, with bright, yellow-painted windows and a cedar door. There was a chimney but no smoke was rising from it. From all appearances, the place looked deserted.

I waited quietly for a few minutes wondering how I could best approach the place without being seen. I decided to walk around to the back, skirting the thick brush of the forest.

Stealthily I made my way, keeping an eye all the while on the quiet house. There was a small back porch with a worn wooden railing. On it, Courtney had placed five flowerpots and from each of them had sprouted healthy-looking greenery. There was a plain wooden door, and a small window—probably the bathroom window.

There was no sign of a car. I wondered about that. If Courtney had driven off somewhere, she'd see my car if she came down Joy Road. Maybe the best thing for me to do would be to go back and hide my car, or park it much farther down the road.

It turned out that I didn't have to make that decision. When I turned around, I was staring down the barrel of a Browning automatic.

"How did you find me, Ken?" Courtney Reed asked.

She was wearing jeans, and a brown suede jacket over a white turtleneck. Her right hand was in a cast that went from her wrist to her elbow. Her left balanced the gun that was pointed at my chest. She had never looked so beautiful . . . or more deadly.

"You weren't terribly difficult to trace. You left the name of your real-estate company in your address book. I followed it up."

She nodded. "That was pretty stupid of me, wasn't it? Who else knows?"

"Why, are you going to kill us all?"

"I'm not killing anyone," she said, emphasizing *I'm*. "I was taking a walk on the road when I saw your car coming up the hill. I waited for you to get out and I followed you. What were you trying to do anyway?"

"Are you going to keep that gun pointed at me?" I asked her.

"That depends. What did you think you were doing?"

"I was going to talk to you. I was going to tell you off, let you know what a bastard I think you are," I said bitterly.

"I'm a bastard?" She underlined the *I'm* again. "You're a sonofabitch! Why couldn't you just leave things alone. We could have had so much but you had to . . . ."

She dropped the gun to her side.

"I had to what?"

"Come on. You know as well as I do."

"What? Spell it out for me."

"Marcano, damn you! Why did you kill him? Did you think you were doing it for me?" she asked sadly.

"I didn't kill Marcano."

She bristled. "You expect me to believe that? You don't have to play to the crowd here, Ken. It's just you and me."

I didn't understand what she was up to. She was turning things around. But why? And she seemed to really mean it. Maybe she was a pathological liar who really believed she was telling the truth.

"What makes you think I killed Orlando?" I asked her quietly.

Her eyes opened wide. "Are you crazy? You called me and told me you were going to kill him. I tried to stop you!"

"When was this?"

"What do you mean, *when?* The night Marcano was killed. Stop trying to confuse me."

She pointed the gun again. "I want you to get out of here. Get in your car and get out of here!"

"If you thought I killed Orlando, why didn't you tell the cops? Why did you run out?"

"I was trying to protect your ass, that's why!"

"And how about Courtney Reed's ass?"

The mention of her real name made her head jerk as if she'd been hit by a Sugar Ray jab.

"Oh, God," she sighed.

Her eyes closed and her knees seemed to buckle. I reached out to steady her. She didn't fight when I took the gun from her hand. I broke it open. It wasn't loaded.

"Let's go inside," I told her.

She nodded slowly and walked shakily to her door.

The Eaton house was furnished in Early Americana. The living room had straight-backed rockers and heavy oak tables. On the walls were muskets, Civil War maps, and a captain's wheel from an old Yankee clipper.

"Do you want a drink?" she asked dully.

"No, but you go ahead."

"I think I could use a cup of strong coffee," she said.

"I'll join you in that."

■ CHAPTER **20** We walked into a bright kitchen
with flowered wallpaper and ging-
ham curtains. I sat at the table
while Courtney put the coffee on.

"How much do you know about Courtney Reed?" she
asked me.

"Armed robbery, accessory to murder . . ."

Her back was to me and I could see her whole body seem to
sag. After a moment, she began measuring the coffee again.

"Do you also know that all of that happened when I was
sixteen years old?" Her voice sounded tired and bitter.

"I really don't know all the details."

"I was sixteen and living with people who'd taken me out
of an orphanage. They had a small farm in Georgia. I was so
happy I was going to be living with a nice family. What I
didn't know was that they raised me not because they wanted
a daughter as much as they wanted cheap labor on their farm.
I wasn't their child, I was their slave. There wasn't anything I
could do about it. When I was fifteen, I ran away for six days.
The Georgia Highway Patrol picked me up and brought me
back. Alice, that's my adopted mother, whipped me so bad
with a razor strop that I couldn't stand up for four days. My
adopted father got real angry. I could hear them arguing. He
said, 'Why'd you whip her so damn hard for? Now I got to git
up early and do the damn milkin'.'"

"What about Gloria?"

"You know my sister?"

"I spoke to her."

"Gloria was all right, but what could she do? They were
working her skinny butt off, too. But at least they weren't
always mean to her. I never heard a kind word from those
people. There wasn't one night that'd go by when I wasn't
crying my eyes out. The only time I was allowed out of the
house was when I went to school, and if they could have gotten away with it, they would have stopped that, too.

"On the way home one day, a man offered me a ride. I
wasn't allowed to accept rides from strangers, so naturally I
did it just for spite. Every day this fellow, John, would come

along in his shiny new car and drive me back to my prison. We started talking about ourselves and he told me he was a salesman and he was going to be in Rome, Georgia, for another week and then he was heading for Florida. He told me I could go with him. He said that if he had a good trip through the South selling his hardware, maybe we could get married."

"You believed that?"

"Damn, I was only sixteen! I'd gone from an orphanage to being abused and working like a damn slave. I would have run off with the devil if he'd talked nice to me and promised I wouldn't have to go back to that farm."

"What happened?"

"It turned out John—his name was John Jordan—was no salesman. He was an escaped convict. We'd drive into a Seven-Eleven and John'd walk out all smiles with a wad of bills in his pocket. He told me he'd made a big sale. What he'd really done was rob the place. I didn't know anything about it, but I was the one driving the car. I had no idea that John was on a three-state crime spree."

"When did you find out?"

"The day some store owner came running out of his place shooting at us with a shotgun. John tried to bluff me with a story but then he finally told me the truth. He told me I was wanted by the cops as much as he was. That night we checked into a motel and while he was in the bathroom, I thumbed my way out of there."

"You could have gone to the police and explained."

"Who was going to believe me? Even if they had, I'd just have been sent back to the farm. Then I read in the paper that one of the people John had held up had been shot and killed. I knew I couldn't go to the police. I got up money for a bus ticket out West and wound up in New Mexico. I always loved to ride so I started mucking stalls on the track. I went from that to exercise girl and then I became a jockey."

"As Tricia Martin?"

"She was some girl I read about in a newspaper. She had gotten killed in an auto accident. She was just about my age and I remember thinking I wished it had been me instead of her. I just borrowed her name."

"You didn't have a problem getting a license or proving who you were?" I asked skeptically.

"I did whatever I had to do," she snapped.

She poured us both cups of coffee. I took mine black, and so did she. She sat down at the table across from me. She seemed drained.

"So you've lived your life as Tricia ever since."

"I didn't have a life as Courtney."

"And John?"

She shrugged. "I never heard another thing, and I didn't want to know anything. Up until recently, I thought that part of my life was dead and buried."

The coffee tasted good. I took a long sip and placed the cup on the table. Courtney fidgeted with its handle.

"There were times when I thought I'd go back and straighten everything out, but I knew it'd be the end of my riding career. That was something I couldn't give up. Then I met you, and I thought maybe things were finally breaking my way . . . but you turned out to be another Johnny Jordan."

"I didn't kill Marcano," I insisted.

"Sure."

"All I know is that someone tried very hard to set me up to take the heat. The most likely person to form the frame was you. You could have gotten my keys, you could have taken my shirt and my watch . . ."

"Me! Why would I do that?"

"Come on. You've got me so mixed up I have no idea what you would or wouldn't do. I'm not even sure who you really are. Courtney . . . or Karen . . . or Tricia."

"And what about your call to me at the hospital?" she snapped. "You told me you were going to kill Marcano!"

"That's not true! That call wasn't from me. It was part of the frame!"

"It *is* true! I tried calling you back but you had already left. I got out of my hospital bed to try and stop you."

"That's why you went to Marcano's house?"

"Yes!"

"Then why did you go home first? The car service driver said he took you to your house where you picked up a small bag."

"I went to get my car," she explained. "I didn't want the driver to see me try and stop you. I didn't want you all over the newspapers again. My house is on the way so I went to get my car. I thought I could manage the stick shift, but I couldn't. I was forced to keep the rented car but I made him park away from Marcano's house."

"And what was in the bag?"

"While I was at my house, I tossed in a pair of jeans and the sweater I'm wearing now. I also took some lipstick and my makeup case. What did you think I took? Your stupid watch and shirt?"

"I don't know."

Everything she said made sense, but . . .

"Why didn't you tell me you had been dating Marcano?" I asked defensively.

"I *had* to date Marcano. I didn't want to, and then I was ashamed to tell you. Okay?"

"Had to? Why? So you could have a chance to ride his stock?" I said bitterly.

"No, I did it for Demaret."

"Demaret? What's he have to do with this?"

"Art Demaret found out, somehow, about John Jordan and me. He threatened to expose me if I didn't help him. He was obsessed with trying to nail Marcano and discover how he was doctoring his horses. All he wanted me to do was to get close to Marcano and get the information and report back."

"How long did that go on?"

"Not long. I went out with Marcano less than a month and I couldn't find anything out. Then you and I got friendly and I told Art that I couldn't do it anymore."

"Demaret was going to let you just walk away?"

"Yes. He turned out to be very nice. He told me he'd find some other way to catch Orlando. He was the one who warned me that the police were going to question me and that they might find out about my past."

"That's why you ran out of the hospital," I said, thinking out loud.

"That, and the fact that Art had told me the police had picked you up for the murder. I was afraid they'd ask me about your phone call threatening to kill Orlando."

"Listen, Trish—Courtney. You're going to have to believe me. The only time I called you was the next morning. I was awakened myself by a caller who said he or she could

135

expose Marcano. That's how they drew me out of my house. Are you sure it was my voice?"

She nodded. "Definitely. It really bothered me the next morning when you called as if nothing had happened. I couldn't believe anyone could be so cold."

She paused. "There was something, though. You sounded kind of funny, like you were drugged."

Now, thinking back on it, I remembered how odd she had sounded when I called her that morning. As if she was waiting for me to say something.

In spite of my inner warnings, I was buying her story.

"Let me understand this. You got a call, like I did, in the middle of the night. You thought you heard my voice and I told you that I was going to kill Orlando."

"I could never forget it. You—or someone who sounded exactly like you—said, 'I'm going to kill Marcano' and then hung up. I tried calling you back at your apartment but you weren't there. I guess I just panicked. I called a car service, stopped off at my house for my car, and then I went to Marcano's."

"What happened when you got there?"

"Nothing. Absolutely nothing. The house was dark and I didn't see your car. I waited a couple of minutes, then I rang the doorbell. There was no answer. I tried looking through the window on the porch and as far as I could see, everything looked completely normal. After a while, I figured that you must have been drunk or something. At any rate, whatever you were going to do, it wasn't going to happen that night."

"Then what happened?"

"Then I had the driver take me back to the hospital. The next morning Bobby called to give me the news about Orlando."

"How did he sound?"

"Very upset. He was a lot more composed when I saw him later."

"He came to the hospital?"

"Just for a couple of minutes to look in on me. After that, you called. I wanted to talk to you but the way you sounded, it was obvious that you didn't want to discuss anything on the phone."

"When did you see Demaret?"

136

"He came in a few minutes after your call. He told me that he had spoken to a detective and that they were going to pick you up for questioning. He asked me if I knew anything at all about what might have happened to Marcano. He kind of looked at me like he thought I might be involved somehow. I told him I had no idea what had happened to Orlando. He told me that with my background, I'd better not lie. He said he'd do whatever he could to help me, but I'd better level with the detectives."

Outside, the snow that had been threatening all day fell from the sky in large powdery flakes.

I wanted to believe her. Her recounting of the events were possible. They even sounded plausible. Yet there was still that nagging doubt. Who else could have set me up if not her?

"What are you going to do now?" I asked her.

She shrugged her shoulders. "I'm tired of running from one place to another. I'm tired of living in fear that someone is going to find me out."

"Stay here for a while. Maybe there's something we can do."

She gave me a long look. "I believe you, Ken. I believe you didn't kill Orlando. Do you believe me?"

"I want to, but I don't know."

She looked sad and I wanted to reach out and hold her in my arms. Instead, I got up and watched the falling snow.

"I haven't asked you this before, and maybe you might feel it's none of my business . . ."

She saw my hesitation.

"You can ask me anything you want," she said.

"Just what kind of relationship did you have with Bob Diamond?"

She gave me a half-smile. "Bobby is just a good friend. If you're really asking me if I ever went to bed with him, the answer is no."

She stared at me, trying to tell if her answer had pleased me. It did, but I tried not to show it.

"What kind of relationship did he have with Marcano?" I asked her.

"Why?" Her eyes narrowed. "You don't think Bobby had anything to do with—"

"I told you before, I don't know. I heard that Marcano was thinking of taking him off his stock permanently."

Courtney played with a lock of her hair, weighing her words carefully. "I'm no snitch, Ken."

"This has nothing to do with snitching. It's between us. It's important!"

She took a deep breath. "I guess you're right," she stated slowly, but then her words quickened. "Bobby was always talking about Orlando. He said that no matter what he did, Orlando would find fault with him. Orlando expected every horse he saddled to be a winner. If they didn't win, he blamed Bobby. Bobby said Orlando was having some big money problems and he was putting pressure on everybody in the stable. I guess you could say Bobby was ticked off."

"Did he ever threaten to do anything about it?"

"Ken, Bobby and I used to talk a lot. You sometimes say things that you don't really mean. You know the way Bobby is, he couldn't hurt a fly."

He sure could have when he'd put his gun to me outside of Courtney's place in Queens. That Bobby had seemed cool and dangerous.

"Ken, it was no secret that they were having problems. Everybody at Marcano's stable knew it. Bobby was especially sore because he was in the best form of his career. He said things the way we all do, but I never took him seriously for one moment."

I nodded. The Bob Diamond I knew was a hard-working journeyman jockey who for the first time in his life was getting a taste of the spotlight. The fact that Marcano might have wanted to replace him didn't seem a strong enough motive for the Texas native to kill anyone. Of course, Bob wasn't the easiest person in the world to get a read on.

In just the few minutes we had been talking, the snow had covered the ground. I walked toward the door.

"You could stay for a while," she said.

We both knew that if I did we'd spend the rest of the day in bed. As much as I wanted to, I needed more time, and perhaps more facts.

"I think I'd better get back. Do you have a phone number here?"

She reached for a piece of note paper with the phone

number of the Eaton residence. I looked at the number she had given me before pocketing it.

"You're not going to run off again?"

She smiled sadly. "No. No more running." She touched my sleeve. "Ken, I'm sorry I didn't have faith in you. I should have known you couldn't do anything so horrible. Do you forgive me?"

"There's nothing to forgive. After all, that phoney call would have been hard for anyone to ignore. Let's face it. I wasn't thinking such nice thoughts about you either."

"Maybe we can gain each other's confidence back now. I want your trust more than anything in the world. We had something special, Ken. I've been around enough to know. You've been the best thing in my life," she said, her eyes moistening. "Ken, please believe me. I had nothing to do with Orlando's death."

"I do believe you," I said.

But even as I said it, something was trying to break through the edge of my consciousness. It was the same feeling you got trying to remember a name or a fact and just as you almost had it, it would slip away.

"Well, I guess I'd better get going, otherwise I could get stuck."

■ CHAPTER  The feeling haunted me all the way home. I kept going over my conversation with Courtney, hoping it would trigger whatever it was that was bothering me, but it was no use.

Just as I was about to put it down as hopeless, I figured it out. I had spent a lot of time in hospitals, unfortunately, and I knew that they shut down their switchboards late at night. How, then, had Courtney gotten a call from me?

I made a quick exit off the thruway at Exit 9, Tarrytown, and stopped at a Howard Johnson's on the service road. Once again the feeling that I had been made a complete fool of surfaced and had me simmering. I found a pay phone in the lobby, stuffed it with change, and punched in Courtney's upstate number.

"Courtney?"

"Ken?" There was concern in her voice. "Are you okay? Did something happen to your car?"

I assured her that I was fine and fought back my anger.

"There was something that you said that started me thinking. Don't hospitals cut off incoming calls at nine or ten P.M.?"

"Yes . . . but—"

"Then maybe you can explain how it was possible for you to get a call from me in the middle of the night?"

"I'd be happy to, if you'd stop screaming in my ear," she said sharply. "I asked them to make an exception in my case. My agent had been out of town and I knew he'd be going crazy until he spoke to me. I told the nursing staff that he had a bad heart and the worrying might kill him. I asked them to do me a favor and call me to the phone in case he called. I helped my argument along with a couple of fifties here and there."

"So they called you to the nurses' station when the call came in?"

"Yes, I guess they assumed it was Mike."

"That's easy enough to check," I warned her.

"Then check it," she said with annoyance.

There was a click as she hung up on me.

I decided that if Courtney was lying, she was the best there was.

I walked over to the desk and broke a bill for some quarters. This time I called the hospital and waited about three minutes while they paged Dr. Ackerman.

"Ken? How are you?" he asked warmly.

"It seems I'm in need of another favor."

"No problem. As a matter of fact, I'm getting a kick out of my sleuthing. What do you want to know?"

"Can a patient get a phone call in the middle of the night?" I asked him.

"Hmmm. Generally, the switchboard is turned off at nine-thirty, though they'll make an exception in an emergency situation. Why? Do you want me to arrange something for a friend of yours?"

"No, nothing like that. I just need you to find out if Cour—I mean, Tricia Martin, got a call the night before she left the hospital. She says a call came in after one A.M. I'd try to run it down myself, but I think the hospital staff would be more inclined to level if you did the asking, especially if it turns out that they got some money under the table."

"You want to hold on? It may take a little while. I'm going to have to track down the charts and see who was around that night."

"I hate to pull you away from your patients."

"Relax, I'm a radiologist. Most of my cases don't require around-the-clock attention. All I have to do is look at the pictures and give an opinion. Give me a number where I can reach you."

I gave him my home number and told him he could leave a message on my machine if I wasn't home.

"Bob, I really appreciate this," I told him.

"Don't worry. I don't mind having my hooks in you for a couple of favors down the road. If tickets are difficult to get for this year's Breeders' Cup, I'll know where to reach you."

■ The storm, which had already dropped about three inches on the ground, was tapering off to intermittent flurries. Crossing into the city over the George Washington Bridge, I started a yawn that didn't end until I hit the Harlem River Drive. As usual, that artery was packed so I took the city streets on my trip downtown. After another bout of yawning, it dawned on me that if I didn't get a dose of caffeine in my system, I was going to conk out at the wheel.

I pulled into a diner's parking lot and used the outside phone. It was about forty minutes since I had spoken to Bob. That should have given him enough time to do his "sleuthing."

My phone rang the prescribed amount of times and I waited patiently for the start of my message before punching in the remote-retrieval code. Bob's was the second message.

The first was from Gus angrily berating me for never being around when he called. He was having lunch with Arlene (I noticed it was *Arlene* now, not Ms. Kirshbaum, or the attorney), and if I could join them, they'd be at P. J. Clark's on Fifty-fifth around two. I checked my watch. If I didn't hit heavy traffic, I could still make it.

"Hi, Ken." Bob's voice came on. "I don't know if this is

one of those thirty-second things, so I'll talk fast. You were right in not poking around yourself. I had a hell of a time finding someone who'd admit to knowing anything about Miss Martin getting a call. However, I kept giving it the old college try, and finally I got a confirmation. She said she was expecting a call from someone and it was an emergency because this guy was very sick, or something like that. The bottom line is that they called her out to the nurses' station well after midnight. I hope this helps you. 'Bye.''

I hadn't realized that I had been holding my breath as Bob spoke. I exhaled slowly.

Courtney hadn't lied. Even though it wasn't me, someone had called her. It was obviously part of the frame-up, but Marcano's killer could not have anticipated that Courtney would take off rather than incriminate me.

I patted myself down for some change in order to call and apologize. Then I thought better of it. I had been kind of blunt on the phone, and decided it would be a good idea to let her cool off.

Two cups of coffee and two pieces of dry toast later, I was back in the car heading toward P. J.'s.

I spotted Gus pacing in front of the entrance looking for all the world like an expectant father. His face broke into a broad smile when he saw me.

"You're impossible to reach, do you know that? I was wondering if you'd ever get my message."

"You're not exactly a shut-in yourself," I told him. "Where's Arlene?"

"She's already inside. I just came out for a second to see if I could spot you. I'm sorry about Courtney Reed, and the knife under her bed. I would have rather told you about that in person, but who knew when I'd see you?"

"Don't worry about it. I just came from talking to her."

"You what?"

"Come on, let's find Arlene and I'll fill you both in."

Arlene was sitting in a booth sipping a martini. She stood up and bussed me, then slid over on the long bench to make room for Gus. I sat opposite the lovebirds. It was surprising to see how much younger and lovelier Arlene looked. The relationship with Gus was obviously agreeing with her.

"How did your hunch pan out?" she asked me.

"I just this minute got back from talking to Courtney."

Gus gave Arlene a puzzled look. "Wait a second!" he said to her. "You knew about this, too. What am I, the only person who doesn't know what's going on?"

"Lawyer-client privilege, dear. Ken and I both decided we didn't want you to worry. What happened?"

I shrugged my shoulders. "I'm sorry, guys. I believe her."

"You believe her!" Gus exploded. You are the most naive—"

"I know," I interrupted. "The fact is that she explained everything and I'm really convinced she's innocent."

"Women can be very shrewd, Ken," Arlene offered. "I just hope you're not wearing blinders."

"Blinkers," I corrected her. "And I don't think so."

We ordered, and I spent most of the next half-hour filling them in on what had happened between forkfuls of salad. I ended by telling them about my message from Dr. Ackerman.

Arlene and Gus listened quietly.

At first, Gus's disgusted expressions showed that he mistrusted Courtney but when I'd finished, he seemed to be coming around.

Arlene looked very thoughtful. "For whatever it's worth, her story about John Jordan seems to be in line with the information I'm receiving from Georgia. He was a very smooth character, I'm told. He had a history of picking up young girls and getting them involved in his holdups."

"How much trouble is Courtney in as a result of that?" I asked.

"It's hard to say right now. We're talking about a case that's been buried for ten years. We're also tiptoeing around it to avoid attracting too much attention. If, however, the story she told you checks out all the way, I think she might get off with very light time or a few years probation. I'm going to stress the *if* part. There might be something we don't know yet that would cancel all bets."

"Hey, hold up for a second," Gus chimed in. "I don't want to be a party pooper here, but what about the knife that popped out from under her hospital bed?"

"That could have been planted by someone who came to visit her. All they had to do was wait for the right moment, reach underneath, and stick the knife in the mattress."

"Yeah, but Ken, a lot of people visited her . . . including me and you," Gus said.

I looked at both of them. "I think we can pin it down. I have two suspects in mind. The first one is Bobby Diamond."

"Diamond? That's the jockey who rode for Marcano," Arlene said.

"Yes. He and Marcano seemed to have had bad blood between them. From what I hear, Marcano was going to put another jockey on his horses, probably Courtney."

"I can't believe that of Bobby," Gus said shaking his head.

"Quite frankly, Gus, from the little I know now, neither can I. Yet, he had a motive and he could have worked the frame as easily as Courtney."

"I see you've already dismissed the lady as a suspect," Gus sighed.

"One-track mind," Arlene smiled and patted Gus's hand. "Who qualifies as your second suspect?"

"Art Demaret."

"Demaret? From track security? Ken, are you crazy?" Gus wanted to know.

"What do you base it on?" Arlene asked.

"He had some strong motives." I counted them off on my fingers. "He was worried about losing his job, and Marcano was making a complete fool out of him and his staff. He blackmailed Courtney into working for him. He was totally obsessed with trying to catch Marcano. If Marcano was dead, he might feel all his problems would be solved."

"You could look at it that way, or you could say that with Marcano dead, there went Demaret's chance at vindication," Arlene suggested.

"He was one of the last people to visit Courtney before the knife was discovered," I countered.

"Sure, but there's no way to determine how long it had been planted there," Gus said.

"Gus, I know that. I'm just trying to come up with a list of people who might have hid the knife under the bed."

"Well, then to be completely fair, Ken, we shouldn't leave out Courtney. She *is* the most obvious. If she did kill Marcano, she could have put the knife in her bag and then . . ."

"She could have, but she didn't. Look, for the sake of

argument, someone could say I did it. Years ago, when I had problems with alcohol and drugs, I had brief periods where I blacked out. I could swear I didn't call Courtney at the hospital that night, but who's to say I didn't experience a blackout of some kind and—"

"But that's ridiculous! The problems you had were so many years ago!"

"Gus, there've been cases of people having drug flashbacks after a decade."

Arlene smiled knowingly. "Every once in a while, that argument is used in court by a defense attorney trying to get his client off. It usually doesn't hold much water. The fact is, Ken, that aside from your personal feelings, Courtney Reed is a logical candidate for your little list. In cases like this, it doesn't hurt to have Gus's Missouri approach."

"That's right!" Gus agreed.

"Gus dear, if you'll just slip out of the booth for a second, I'll be able to get to the ladies room," Arlene told him.

"Sure," he said.

As soon as Arlene was out of earshot he turned to me. "Hey, Ken, what the hell's she talking about? I don't come from Missouri."

■ CHAPTER  My next stop was Art Demaret's office at the racetrack. It was almost post time for the Eighth Race feature and Nancy, Demaret's secretary, told me the boss was watching the race from the third floor in the clubhouse. "He usually sits in Mr. Kiltman's box."

I thanked her and rode the elevator to the owners' boxes and drew a bead on Demaret. He was sitting up close to the rail, four tickets firmly clutched in his right hand.

The horses were coming around the turn and down the homestretch. I spotted the silks of the stable Joe Herrera trained for. Tony Violet was in there pinch-hitting for me and he had the lead. With forty yards to go, a horse closed a lot of ground on the outside. Violet and the other jock, J.J. Alvarado, were in a furious whipping, driving finish. The winner would have to be ascertained by a photograph.

The people in the owners' boxes looked down at the finish line from a spot fifteen yards or so past the wire. I knew that the angle from this vantage point in any close finish made it seem that the inside horse had won. Since this race appeared to be a tie, even with the angle bias, in my opinion this was one finish Violet would come out of on the short end.

One of the owners with whom I had a nodding acquaintance called out to me. "How did you see it, Eagle?"

"I'd have to say it was the 'eight.'" I identified the horse farthest from the rail.

Demaret looked back from the first row. "I hope you're wrong, Eagle. I think Violet got him home on the inside with the last bob."

We all stared at the toteboard. Upstairs, the stewards were reviewing the photo. The placing judge would be calling down the results to the computer technician who controlled the infield tote.

The sign lit up OFFICIAL. The final order of finish was 8—5—7—1.

Demaret ripped up his tickets and tossed them over his shoulder. "If you'd been riding, Eagle, you would have nailed it on the wire," he said.

It wasn't true. Tony Violet's strength was his ability to bring a horse home, but I accepted Demaret's compliment with a smile.

"May I have a brief word with you, Art?" I asked him.

"Sure. How about a cup of coffee in the cafeteria—that is, if I can still afford it after that race."

There was a lot to be learned about human nature in any racetrack's cafeteria. In the early morning, handicappers with their *Daily Racing Forms,* chart books, pocket calculators, Ouija boards and horoscopes, sat hunched over the tables busily plotting their course to the cashier's window. These were basically loners, generally strong-willed individuals who were comfortable making their own choices and if need be, going against the tide of popular opinion. They were emotionally weatherbeaten men who had braved the storms of bad racing luck and had known the ups and downs of victory and defeat. The fact that the same people returned day after day, month after month, and year after year, gave testimony to their powers of tenacity and survival.

As the clock moved to the First Race (12:30 post time), a different breed came in. These were younger people, some wearing trade uniforms who'd left their vans in the parking lot as they stole a couple of hours from the job. They hoped to make a killing in the Double, or the Third Race Exacta. They carried tout sheets, lucky number books, dream-analysis reports, and the old standby—the consensus picks of the local newspapers. All barriers of class, race, religion, were broken in the quest for winners. The all-important question that seemed to be on everyone's lips was, "Who ya like?"

There was always an air of excitement and hope. Before the race, everyone was a winner. Everyone had the chance of hitting the Triple, or the Pick Five, and coming home with armored trucks filled with money.

As the day unfolded with each passing race, and the yawning maws of the mutuel machines sucked in the dollars, the crowds in the cafeteria thinned and the mood turned quiet and tense. By three o'clock, there would be a few souls staring into their coffee, making up lies to tell the wife, or trying to figure out a way to get train fare home. The clean floors of the morning would now be littered with worthless stubs, cigarette butts, and printed matter filled with the unrealized predictions of false prophets.

Demaret and I took a table near the cashier and because we were both part of the track family, the manager brought over our coffees and told us they were on the house.

"When's your vacation going to be over?" Demaret asked me.

"In a day or two, I suppose."

"Well, you better get back fast. Your pal, Violet, is making a strong run for the rider's title. I hear if he gets real close, he might do some night racing at Meadowlands."

"That's youth for you," I replied. "The one time I tried doubleheaders, I wound up too weak to hold the reins. I fell off a fifteen-thousand-dollar claimer and spent the next six weeks in the hospital."

"Eighty-one, that happened. The horse's name was Maggie Joe and it was the Ninth Race," Demaret rattled off.

"That's amazing!" I was genuinely impressed.

Demaret smiled. "I've got a good memory. I trained myself to have a good memory. Actually, anyone can do it. It's just a matter of concentrating, but I guess you're not here to discuss my memory, Eagle. So what can I do for you?"

I decided to be up front. "What does the name Courtney Reed mean to you?" I asked him.

He didn't even twitch. "What's it supposed to mean to me?" he asked easily.

"It's the name of a girl who got herself in a little trouble about ten years ago."

Demaret stared at the vapor rising from his cup. "Am I supposed to know about this?"

"Come off it, Art," I said quietly. "I just had a long talk with the girl. She told me that you'd spotted her."

Demaret stared at me dully. Finally, he leaned back in his chair. He made a tent with his fingers. "I guess I should have reported her as soon as I made her as Courtney. I didn't, though. I saw a kid who had gotten a pretty bad start and I thought of my own daughter just a couple of years younger than her. Maybe I'm getting soft, Eagle. I decided I wouldn't blow the whistle. I gave her a chance to keep up her masquerade and maybe get somewhere. I think you would have done the same thing."

"You used her to help you investigate Marcano."

"I don't deny it. Look, Ken, there's no free lunch. I scratch your back, you scratch mine. I would have used anyone to trap that Marcano bastard."

"You really hated him, didn't you?"

Demaret laughed. "Yeah, I hated him. I hated him professionally. I hated him the same way I hated the opposing team when I played baseball or football. That nose guard was my enemy. I was trying to get the quarterback and he was trying to protect him. Every week I'd look at the picture of the guy I was going to be playing opposite and I worked myself up into a lather of hate. After the game, I didn't even know who he was. We shook hands, went our separate ways, and I pasted a new guy's picture over my locker."

"Do you mind telling me how you knew who Tricia was?"

Demaret shrugged. "Why should I mind? I was the FBI agent in charge of the Southern regional office. We had been

148

after this John Jordan for months. The jerk wasn't satisfied to stay in one state. As soon as he perpetrated crimes across the state lines, he became a federal offender. The girl's picture came across my desk and we had a bulletin out on her. Mainly, we wanted her to testify against Jordan. In the end we didn't need her because somebody whacked Jordan with a two-by-four in the prison yard.

"Listen, Eagle, maybe you shouldn't be getting involved in this. By the way, how did you know that I used her to help me get close to Marcano?"

"She told me."

"Recently?" he asked, cocking his head.

He reminded me of a big dog trying to pick out a strange sound.

"Yeah, fairly recently. She told me that she came to you and said she wasn't going to spy for you anymore."

"Maybe I told her I didn't need her anymore, or maybe she wanted to quit . . . it doesn't really matter."

"You didn't need her anymore?" I asked incredulously. "Why? You never did figure out Marcano's scam."

"Well, he wasn't going to reveal anything to her, so what the hell. As it turned out, his secret is buried with him."

"No, it's not. Tell your friends in the lab to come up with a test for fentanyl," I told him.

"Oh, fentanyl." He laughed silently to himself. "You armchair detectives really tickle me. Do you think I never thought of fentanyl? I know all about it. I know what it can do for a horse. You know what the problem is with your fentanyl, Mr. Smartass?" Demaret's voice rose with anger.

"Why don't you tell me."

"You need a hypo full of the stuff if you want it to have an immediate effect. And how do you administer it? Me and my men had our eyes on Marcano and everyone else who came in contact with his horse before the race. Or maybe you think we'd miss a hypodermic," he said sarcastically.

"All you would need is a couple of drops."

Demaret sighed. "You want to run that by me again?"

"All you would need is a couple of drops, and the hypo could be as small as a thumbtack."

Demaret stared at me. The mention of the thumbtack had obviously intrigued him.

"You've got my attention, jockey, now let's see if you can hold it. There is such a thing as a tack needle, but how do you get the fentanyl to be so concentrated?"

"It doesn't have to be if it's given in conjunction with a drug called corrasalin. Corrasalin is injected in the horse up to a month before the fentanyl. It acts like a booster."

Demaret took a pen out of his pocket and started writing. I had been carrying the tack needle around with me since leaving Sara's lab. I took it out of my pocket and let Demaret inspect it. He balanced it in his palm, held it to the light and then handed it back.

"How the hell do you know about this stuff? What are you, some kind of chemistry freak?"

"Find the right person to ask the questions, and you wind up with the right answers."

"Is that supposed to be a dig at me?" Demaret asked angrily. "If it is, it's off the mark. I had some of the top people in the country in on this case. That included chemistry professors from—"

"I wasn't riding you, Art. The reason I'm telling you this is so that someone else doesn't do it again."

He thought about that, and finally nodded. "Okay, Eagle. I'll have this corrasalin checked out with the fentanyl. If it turns out to be the jackpot, I owe you a thank you. I . . . I'm sorry if I snapped at you. I have to admit, I've become thin-skinned about this whole Marcano deal. Since you seem to know so much about it, do you have any idea if there was anybody else in on it with Orlando?"

"You checked out all the horses before they went to post. Did Marcano saddle every one?"

It was customary for a trainer to walk out to the paddock with his horse and rider. The trainer would check the saddle straps and the horse's equipment, and give the jockey any last-minute instructions. "Go to the front and then improve your position," was the typical kind of wisdom that trainers imparted. Sometimes a trainer had two horses riding in the same race as a coupled entry, or had out-of-town commitments. When that happened, he'd leave the post-time chores to an appointed assistant. In Marcano's barn, Judge Phil Pearl handled those assignments.

"There were seven races where a Marcano horse came in

150

first or a whiskered second with Pearl saddling the stock," Demaret said, using that memory of his again.

"Maybe they were just superior horses and won without the juice."

Demaret shook his head. "No way! Not those glue-factory rejects. Believe me, Eagle, I got to know the look of a Marcano doped-up special. These horses went to the post with fire in their eyes. It was downright scary to see a placid animal suddenly turn into a demon horse."

"So that would mean an accomplice," I said.

"Not Phil Pearl," Demaret said, shaking his head. "I wouldn't swear for anyone, but he is the least likely to be involved with something shady."

Demaret happened to be right. Phil Pearl was an eighty-year-old black man who had spent his entire life on one backstretch or another. In all that time, you would have been hard pressed to find anyone willing to say a bad word about him. His reputation for honesty had earned him the moniker of "The Judge." It was unthinkable that Phil Pearl might be involved in a fix. That was probably the reason Marcano had hired him.

"That leaves Bob Diamond," I said.

I could almost see the wheels spinning in Demaret's brain.

"That's an interesting notion," he said at last. "Maybe I should talk to him about it. You want to sit in?"

"I do, but maybe it would be best if you talked to him alone."

■ There was a small waiting area that I hadn't noticed before in Demaret's outer office. The nook, with a couple of wooden chairs, a small table, and some weekly magazines, was located just past Nancy's desk near the office's watercooler. I took a seat and waited for Bobby to appear.

Demaret couldn't force Diamond to talk to him. As the track security man, he had no subpoena power. What he did have, however, was the job of policing all that went on on the racetracks belonging to the New York Racing Association. With a force of well over one hundred men at his command, he had more manpower at his disposal than many good-sized towns, or small cities.

151

Demaret was backed in the performing of his duties by the three track stewards. Like umpires in baseball or referees in football, the stewards made judgment calls and upheld the rules. Unlike their counterparts in other sports, the stewards issued rulings and punished infractions that had nothing to do with the actual running of races. For example, they issued fines for profanity. They could suspend you for smoking in shed row, or passing bad checks. If a member of the racing fraternity didn't honor a debt, he could be banned from the track until restitution was made.

Among the various decisions that were made by stewards all over the country was a determination of whether an individual had done anything "detrimental to the sport of racing." If Diamond refused to cooperate with Demaret, the security man could influence the stewards to strip Bobby of his license under the detrimental-to-racing clause. Reciprocal agreements with stewards in other states, as well as other parts of the world, would ensure that Diamond would never race again.

This system of judge and jury had no relation to jurisprudence, but it worked. It was also the reason that Bob Diamond came when he was summoned to Demaret's office.

As usual, he was wearing jeans, a fancy cowboy shirt—red with white stitching and rhinestone studs—and of course, the ever-present Stetson.

"I was summoned by His Majesty," Diamond told Nancy.

He spotted me sitting there. "Hey, Ken, he's got you down here, too?"

"Apparently so," I shrugged.

"Got any idea what it's about?" he asked me as he fished out a small pouch of chewing tobacco from his pants pocket and stuck a pinch in his cheek.

"You can go right in, Mr. Diamond," Nancy told him before I could come up with some sort of answer.

"Sorry to get ahead of you, Ken, but that's the breaks. Thank you, little lady," he told Nancy.

It was typical of Diamond, who stood five-four at most, to call the almost-six-foot Nancy "little lady."

I tried to sort out my mixed feelings about Bobby Diamond. For one thing, he was handsome, with a quality of utmost self-assurance. He had never been anything but friendly and courteous to me in the years that I'd known him.

152

Although Bobby seemed to know everyone, and people were naturally attracted to him, he had no real close friends. Up until recently, I would have thought he was very friendly with Marcano but both Courtney and Demaret had confirmed that the two had grown far apart.

If in fact he had been doping Marcano's horses, then I wanted him to be caught and punished. The sport of racing had originated as a gentlemen's pastime. The wealthy gentry of Europe had been able to support a race without any support from the hoi poloi.

Modern racing, however, was totally dependent on the trust and attendance of the general public. A betting scandal always generated comments such as: "See, you can't win. I told you it was fixed."

Needless to say, if that attitude took hold, there'd be smaller handles, less purse money, fewer horses, fewer tracks, and ultimately fewer jockeys. Since I was a jockey, it was in my interest that the integrity of racing be maintained. If Bob actually had administered the fentanyl, he was a traitor to the men and women, most of them hard-working and decent, whose livelihood could be threatened by his selfish actions.

The voices behind Demaret's glass-paneled office door grew louder and more heated. I could make out who was yelling, but not what was being said.

Nancy and I exchanged glances.

"Sounds like they're having a tiff," she said.

"A tiff? It's more like a war."

Suddenly the door swung open. Diamond stormed out without looking in my direction. He slammed the outer office door behind him.

"Oh, dear," Nancy said.

I knocked on Demaret's door.

"Yeah, come in, Eagle."

Demaret had some balled-up tissue paper in his hand and he was dabbing at an ugly brown stain on his shirt and tie.

"That little sonofabitch spit tobacco juice at me," he said angrily. "He caught me by surprise. I could have wrung his neck."

"I take it he didn't appreciate your line of questioning."

"Yeah, you could say that. He clammed up and wouldn't say a thing."

"Do you want to venture an opinion?" I asked Demaret.

"I'll give you an opinion. Guilty as charged! I've inter-viewed hundreds of suspects during my career and he's as guilty as they come."

"What now?"

"I'm going to contact Vince Fusco. Hang on."

He pushed a button on the intercom. "Nancy, get me Vince Fusco."

He looked up at me. "I'll ask Fusco to get a warrant so we can have a looksee in all of Mr. Diamond's hiding spots. If he's the keeper of the juice, we'll find it," Demaret said positively.

■ I drove back to my apartment alternately feeling like a rat for turning Bob in, angry that he might have been the one who'd tried to frame me, and worried about the extent of Courtney's impending legal problems.

I was calling her when the blinking light on the answering machine caught my attention. I turned the contraption on and Courtney's voice came over loud and clear.

"Hi, Ken. I hope you don't mind, and I hope you don't have other plans, but I miss you terribly and I'm coming over. I was able to rent a car with an automatic transmission, so driving won't be a problem. I hope you're home, and I hope you still care about me."

There was a slight pause. "Because I care about you *very* much," she said huskily.

■ CHAPTER  Whatever resolve I had fortified myself with melted shortly after Courtney walked through my door. Her eyes were red from crying.

"I hated being away from you. A hundred times I wanted to call you and I just stopped myself. I love you, Ken. When I thought you killed Marcano it just brought back John. I thought I loved him and then I found out he'd killed someone. This time was like a crazy déjà vu. I should have known better. I should have known you could never do something like that."

I didn't tell her how deep my suspicions were of her. There was no reason to do so, and it would have been hard to talk while we kissed.

We made love in an almost desperate, clutching way, as if we were both afraid to let go for fear we'd lose each other. It seemed we were both intent on blocking out the events of the past week. Later, I absently caressed the nape of her neck while she lay sleeping, nude under the covers of my bed.

When this was all over, I wanted to get away alone with Courtney Reed. It would be important to have some time together where we could get to know one another without any masks or mysteries about our pasts.

The buzzing of the apartment intercom caught me by surprise.

"Are you expecting anyone?" Courtney mumbled in a sleepy voice.

"No. I'll see who it is," I told her.

I pressed the "talk" button. "What is it, Chester?"

"Two gentlemen here to see you, Mr. Eagle. What did you say your name was? Oh, yeah. It's a Mister Demaret and a Detective Fusco."

I couldn't imagine what they wanted here.

Courtney was standing in the hallway pulling on her blouse over her cast. "Let them in, Ken. I'll stay in the bedroom."

"Okay, Chester, send them up."

I turned to Courtney. "Is it possible they tracked you here?"

She shook her head. "No. It has to be something else." She went back into the room and closed the door.

Fusco and Demaret lumbered into the apartment. There was nothing else in the world that these two could be but cops. They both wore beige raincoats, dark slacks, and drawn expressions.

"We're not going to stay long," Demaret said.

I walked them into the living room and brushed off Fusco's apologies about getting snow on my carpet. I asked them if they wanted something to drink and they both declined.

For a brief moment I wondered if Fusco had discovered some new evidence and I was going to be arrested again.

Then I realized that didn't jibe with their manner or Demaret's comment about not staying long.

"I asked Demaret to come over here with me, Eagle. Since I was the one who hauled you downtown, I think it's only right that I come by here tonight and tell you I'm sorry. We just came from Diamond's house and it looks as if the Marcano case is a wrap."

I exchanged looks with both of them. "I'm sorry, guys. I don't get it. What happened at Bobby's?"

"Diamond's dead," Demaret said bluntly. "He killed himself."

"Yeah, but at least before he pulled the trigger, he had the decency to take responsibility for killing Orlando," Fusco said.

"That's right. He made a big point of saying he was sorry he'd tried to make you the fall guy."

I kept looking from Demaret to Fusco and back again as if I was watching a tennis match.

"I'm not sure I understand what you're telling me," I said finally.

Demaret nodded. "After you left my office, I called Detective Fusco and asked him to meet me at the track. He came to my office, and as I told you I would, I discussed the things you'd brought to my attention. Fusco was able to get a warrant over the phone and we were about to leave my office to look over Diamond's place.

"All of a sudden, Nancy buzzed me. She said Mr. Diamond was on the phone. I took the call and he told me I was right in my suspicions about him doping the horses. He and Marcano were partners and the partnership had gone sour. Marcano was greedy and was always looking for more and more dough. Bobby wanted to be cautious. Diamond said he realized that he could do better without Orlando, so he worked out a plan to get rid of him. He was sorry it was you he chose to pin it on, but he had his reasons. When you popped off at Orlando at the hospital, he figured that was his chance. I told him to tell this to Fusco and I handed the phone to the detective."

Fusco continued the story. "I took the phone from Demaret and the next thing I hear is a bang. I knew immediately the guy had pulled the plug."

"He shot himself?" I asked quietly.

"We went to his house and there he was. He still had his coat and gloves on. He'd never bothered to take them off. He'd just come back to the house for his gun, called us up, and pulled the trigger. The phone was hanging off the table," Demaret told me.

"You might want to know that we found some vials of fentanyl and some other stuff that is probably that corrasalin substance you mentioned to Demaret. We also found this."

Fusco tossed over a set of keys to me. "Match them with your own keys and I guarantee they'll be duplicates. That's how he got your shirt, and if he didn't get your watch out of your apartment, he got it from your locker. You were set up, pal. No question about it."

Demaret stood up and put his hand on my shoulder. "It's over now, Eagle. It's a damn shame it had to be this way."

Fusco rose, too. "There are a few loose ends left to pick up, but I think we'll be able to piece the whole story together now." He took back the set of keys. "Let's just experiment," he said, opening the door.

He tried fitting the key in the lock.

"That won't work. I changed the cylinder." I handed him my old set of keys.

Fusco compared them. "Perfect match," he said.

"You mind if I ask a favor of you, Eagle?" Demaret looked a bit uncomfortable.

"What is it, Art?"

"Well, the fact that you came up with the way the horses were being juiced doesn't do you any good. If I could put in my report that I figured out how it was done, it could mean whether my contract gets renewed or not. If you have a problem with that, I'll understand."

"No, I've got no problem with it."

"Thanks, Eagle. You really are a good guy," he said.

I tapped Fusco on the shoulder. "Detective Fusco, where does this leave Tricia Martin?" I asked.

"You mean Courtney Reed, don't you? I'm not as stupid as I look despite what our friend Ms. Kirshbaum might think. Reed's clear on this Marcano thing but she still has to straighten out some warrants issued on her in a federal court."

"I intend to do everything I can to get the charges dropped," Demaret told me.

He was giving me notice that my helping him would mean him helping Courtney. Art Demaret had told me he was a firm believer in one hand washing the other.

When I was sure they had left, I walked back to Courtney in the bedroom.

"You heard?" I asked her. I was still dazed.

She was sitting on the edge of the bed, staring out the window.

"I just can't believe it," she whispered. "Bobby's dead. He tried to frame you."

I sat down next to her and put my arm around her. We sat like that for a few minutes, both of us lost in our thoughts of Bob Diamond.

"Thank God it's all over," Courtney said. "At least it is over."

■ The celebration dinner party was Gus's idea.

We were ushered to a special table at the Helmsley Palace and treated to one of the most sumptuous meals I had ever eaten.

It was a veal dish that Gus swore I'd be able to square with my scale the next morning. Courtney had the same thing I did, but she cheated with a baked potato smothered in butter.

"I've still got five weeks before this comes off," she said, raising the cast. "I'll work off the calories by then."

"You burn off four hundred calories during sex," Gus told her. "Keep that in mind." He winked.

"I thought it was closer to one hundred," Arlene said.

"Not the way I do it," Gus answered to a chorus of laughs.

We settled back with coffees and for the first time in a long while, I felt happy and relaxed.

"I have a couple of items I'd like to share at this time," Arlene said, smiling warmly. "I spoke to Fusco and as far as the police are concerned, Ken is completely vindicated. Not only that, but I've also been in contact with some of my Southern associates and the word I'm getting is that the federal government might not prosecute Ms. Reed. There may be a hearing, but with some letters attesting to your character, Courtney, I think you can put the past behind you."

Courtney reached over and squeezed Arlene's hand. "I don't know how I can thank you," she said.

Gus picked up his glass of champagne. "Here's to better times coming down the homestretch."

The others joined in the toast. I clinked glasses with the rest of them, even though my glass had only water.

"You know what I don't understand, though, Ken? How did Bobby imitate your voice, and why?" Courtney asked.

"I had to ask Arlene about that myself," I said, looking over at Kirshbaum.

We all waited as the ex-FBI agent and lawyer put down her glass. "We might never know for sure. He could have given the police another anonymous tip that you'd received a mysterious phone call. When the police questioned you, he was sure you would have said it was Ken. It was just another piece of the elaborate frame."

I nodded. "You see, darling, he never thought you would get out of your bed and actually try to head me off. He also had no idea that you would disappear rather than implicate me."

"Don't make me so noble, Ken. I was also running to help myself. I could still swear it was your voice, though."

"It might very well have been. It's a very easy thing to do. All you need is two tape recorders with number counters. Bobby could have taped a conversation with Ken, and then spliced out certain words from one tape and put them on another. That would account for the metallic quality you said the voice had," Arlene explained.

"I also think the reason Bobby made the mistake with the unopened watchband," Arlene continued, "was because you rang the doorbell and peeked through the window of Marcano's house. Bobby was frightened and screwed up. If you hadn't been there, we might not be celebrating here tonight."

"Okay," Gus said, "I got all that part. What I don't understand is why Diamond wanted to stick it to you, Ken. You two never had a fight or anything."

"I figured that out," I told them. "It was Courtney."

"Me?"

159

"I think Bobby was in love with you, too. By pinning Marcano's murder on me, he got rid of his rival."

"But if he was in love with me, why did he plant the knife under my bed?"

"I don't think it was supposed to be discovered there. He couldn't know that the mop head would dislodge it. I think it was there only until he could figure out a way to plant it on me."

"But he was so nice," Courtney said wistfully.

"Sometimes it's hard to tell the good guys from the bad guys," I said.

"Amen!" Arlene chimed in agreement.

■ CHAPTER **24** I pulled up in front of Courtney's house and started to park in her driveway.

"Ken, would you be very angry with me if I didn't invite you in?" she asked.

I looked at her questioningly. "Are you okay?"

"Maybe it's the champagne, but I have a terrible headache and I'm just so tired."

"Headache? We're not even engaged yet," I kidded. "Sure, no problem. You get a good night's sleep and I'm sure you'll feel better in the morning."

I stayed until she found her keys in her bag. I gave her a good-night kiss and then walked back to the car.

In a way I was glad that Courtney was going to sleep early. It meant I could sack out myself and get a good start in the morning. I decided I would get to the track tomorrow and start exercising some horses in order to get back in riding shape. A few days exercising Herrera's stock and I would be ready to go full tilt in the afternoon minus the two or three pounds I had picked up during my "vacation."

It was going to be harder for Courtney to get back into the swing of things, especially if she kept eating baked potatoes with butter. I smiled to myself.

Court said the cast was coming off in five weeks. That

could mean at least another month before the hand and arm were in good enough shape to ride. It was a real shame that the fall had happened just when Courtney was hitting her full stride as a professional jockey.

Unbidden, her fall off Telno came to mind in detail and with perfect clarity. Courtney had almost been killed. It was pure luck that she was all right. And Telno? That veteran campaigner had had to be destroyed because Bobby and Orlando . . .

The suddenness of the realization made me jam on the brake to avoid hitting the car in front of me. Something was wrong! It just didn't make sense.

I ignored the horns and curses of the other motorists and turned my car around in the direction of Courtney's house. There had to be an explanation and Courtney—I hoped— would be able to supply it.

I pulled into her driveway and walked up to the door. I wondered if I was making a fool out of myself and then I put that thought out of my head. I knew I wasn't going to sleep until I'd resolved this, so it might as well be now.

I tried the bell and then I used the heavy brass knocker in case she was sleeping and didn't hear the bell. She wasn't sleeping.

"Ken! What are you doing back here?" she asked surprised.

She was still wearing the beige outfit she had worn to dinner.

"We have to talk," I told her. "Aren't you going to ask me in?"

"What . . . oh yes. Of course."

I followed her into the living room. There was a small fire burning and the room was warm and inviting.

"Sit down, Ken, and tell me what this is all about. You look very upset."

I sat next to her on the sofa. "I was on the way home and for some reason, I thought about the fall you took on Telno."

"That shouldn't have upset you. I'm fine now. Was it some kind of delayed reaction?" She reached out and held my hand.

"No, it's something else. Look, Court, Marcano didn't saddle Telno. He was in the trustees' room for some reason."

"That's right. He was being interviewed by some cable station. Phil Pearl gave me a leg up, so what about it?"

161

"Bobby Diamond was on suspension," I told her.

"Of course he was on suspension, silly. That's the reason I was riding. What are you trying to say, darling?"

"Don't you see, Court? If Marcano wasn't there, and Bobby wasn't there, who injected the horse?"

Courtney stared at me blankly. She shrugged her shoulders. "No one did. I guess Telno wasn't given anything."

"He was tanked up, all right. I know that horse. I rode him myself at least six or seven times in his career. He was flying before he went down. He moved past me like I was stuck in first gear."

"Superior jockey on the horse," Courtney said, smiling.

"Court, this is serious."

"What's serious? Horses get good all of a sudden. Telno came to hand, that's all."

"No!" I insisted. "That horse was drugged. You were on his back. You must have felt something different about him."

"Honestly, I didn't, Ken. I remember that he made a nice move, but I didn't think it was anything remarkable. I've been on lots of horses who—"

"Not like that! And certainly not on Telno. Tomorrow, I'll get the tapes of that race and check it."

"Ken, why are you so obsessed with this?" she asked with a puzzled look on her face.

"Don't you understand? If it wasn't Marcano or Bobby who gave Telno the fentanyl, it had to be someone else. That means someone else was in on it."

Courtney reached out and took my hand. "Ken, can't we forget about this stuff for now? I want you to come upstairs with me and throw me down on the bed and—"

"Courtney, stop!" I stood up. "Don't you see how important this is?"

"No. No, I really don't! I don't care if one person or ten people were involved in some stupid betting scheme. Whatever they did, it's none of my business and none of yours. It's over. Bobby's dead and it's over!"

I looked at her. She was more beautiful than a woman had a right to be.

"Come on, Ken," she smiled. "There's a fire going, you and me, a nice cozy couch. Maybe we don't need to go upstairs." She started to unbutton her blouse.

It came to me out of the blue. *"Demaret!"* I yelled.

"What?"

"Art Demaret. He was always around every Marcano horse. It had to be him!"

"Ken, that's ridiculous."

"No. No! It makes perfect sense," I said excitedly. "No one watched Demaret. He kept everybody away from Marcano and his horses. He insisted on giving them last-minute clearance himself. It would be the easiest thing in the world for him to inject them with fentanyl."

"But Bobby did it! You heard what Fusco said. He confessed."

"Fusco didn't hear the confession. Demaret told Fusco what Bobby had said."

"Ken, please, this whole thing has me very confused. Can't we just drop it?"

I hardly heard her.

"Court, how do we know Bobby was involved at all? Demaret had the same access as Diamond to my locker. He could have been the one who stole my keys. He could have just as easily been the one who played that tape to fool you in the hospital. That whole business about Bob and Orlando having a falling out . . . . What if the facts were true but instead of Diamond, it was Demaret?"

"Ken, Art Demaret wouldn't do that. You can't implicate him in this. He's a good guy. He could have called the police when he first spotted me, but he didn't. He's promised to help me when I go to the federal hearing."

"But, Courtney, he may have killed Bobby!"

"Bobby committed suicide!"

"Did he? What did Demaret say? He was still wearing his coat and gloves. How convenient that he was wearing gloves so there would be no powder burns on his hand. There's only one problem."

I sat back down on the sofa and leaned my head back.

Courtney put her head on my shoulder. "And what might that be?" she asked softly.

"Nancy. Demaret's secretary. She buzzed Demaret with Fusco sitting there and said she had a call from Diamond. She knew him well enough to recognize his Texas drawl."

Courtney was kissing me, little baby kisses running up and down my cheek. "What does that mean?"

I thought about Bobby in the waiting room outside Demaret's office. I thought of the brown stain on Demaret's shirt where Bobby had spit on him. There had been something wrong right from the first about Diamond's supposed suicide. That just wasn't Bobby.

"It means Bobby was murdered . . . but not by Demaret. Fusco did hear the actual shot, and Nancy really did hear Bobby's voice."

"Who did it, darling?" she said, putting her free arm around my neck and giving me a long hard kiss that left me panting.

"I don't know," I whispered.

"Yes, you do," she said, kissing me again.

Her fingers were undoing the buttons of my shirt. She reached down for my belt. I was aware of her body close to mine, her hot breath on my face.

I reached out and pushed her back. "You," I whispered, and I knew it was true.

"Make love to me, Ken. I need you to make love to me," she breathed.

I held her back. Our eyes locked onto one another's. "Did you kill Marcano, too?"

"Yes," she purred.

She smiled at me. It was a slow, evil smile. "What are you going to do about it?" she asked.

"You *and* Demaret. You both set me up."

"That was our intention. I'm glad it didn't work out that way. This is much neater. Bobby gets the rap and we don't have to worry about him coming up with new evidence. We've made a lot of money, Ken, and some of it belongs to you . . . if you'll keep your mouth shut."

"You must be crazy!" I told her.

"Sure, I'm crazy. I lost ten years of my life living in fear and pretending to be someone I wasn't. I can have it all now! I can have it all . . . and you, too."

"Not me!"

"Yes, you. You're in love with me. You know you'll never meet another woman like me. You know there isn't another person in the world who is as perfect for you as I am. Yes, I

164

murdered and I lied, and I tried to set you up, but in the end you're going to forgive me. No one has to know, darling." She was so sure of me, so damn sure.

"I'll know."

"Over time you'll forget. The bad memories will fade. You have to believe me, Ken. I didn't love you at first. I was ready to use you, to frame you. Later on, I really fell in love with you. You're not going to throw that away. I know you're not."

I nodded slowly. "You're right. I'm helplessly in love with Trish and Courtney. I could never do anything to hurt them."

"I know that, darling."

"My only problem is I have no idea who *you* are."

"What does that mean?"

"That means you can save your breath. I'm going to call the police."

I began walking toward the door.

"Please, darling, don't," she called.

I didn't listen.

There was a precinct about five blocks away. I was going to go there, call Fusco, and tell him everything I knew.

"Touch that doorknob and I'll shoot you right here!" a male voice warned.

I spun around.

Art Demaret had stepped out from the small hall that led to the kitchen. He walked into the living room and took a seat next to Courtney. A large revolver was in his hand.

It was aimed at my head.

■ CHAPTER 25 I was ordered to take a seat on the chair facing them. I didn't know much about guns, but this one had a mean snub nose and at this range, Demaret could have closed his eyes and he wouldn't have missed. Even if I'd had the inclination, it was no time for heroics.

Courtney took the gun from Demaret.

"Finish splitting the money," she told him. "I'll keep him here until you come back."

Demaret gave me an angry glare.

"You really weren't thinking about splitting with him, were you?" he asked her.

"What do you think, Art?"

"I think you were playing cat and mouse," he said.

"You're wrong. If he had told me he would have kept his mouth shut, I'd have believed him. I meant everything I said, Ken. Every word." She smiled, shaking her head. "You don't know how sorry I am, Ken, that you couldn't have made the right choice. Get going, Art. I don't want to stretch this out any more than I have to."

Demaret got up slowly. He was going to say something to Courtney but then thought better of it. He walked through the hall into the kitchen. It was obvious that she was the one running this show.

I still had trouble believing this beautiful, talented woman who I had fallen in love with was a murderess.

"Why, Court? Why did you do it?"

"You couldn't understand," she said simply.

"Try me. You had everything going for you. Your career was taking off. You were riding well . . ."

She gave it a few moments thought. "When I woke up in the hospital I realized that I'd come within an inch of dying. I got to thinking, Ken, about how I had wasted my life. I had been cheated of everything, even when I was a baby. I saw it as another chance, call it a second chance, at life and I was going to have it all this time.

"When you popped off in the newspaper, well . . . that made the timing perfect. Mr. No Guts over there was supposed to do it, but he chickened out at the last minute. I had to get out of the damn hospital and take care of Orlando. I don't feel too bad about that, though. He deserved it, the pig."

"So the call that came into the hospital was—"

"Demaret, saying he was chickening out, but I wasn't going to let the opportunity slip away. It would have worked, too, except for that damn watchband. I had been moving around too much and the fingers on my cast hand got numb. I couldn't unhook the damn band with one hand. It took me so long, I finally just stuck it in Marcano's hand and took off. I got so flustered I even walked out of there with that stupid knife. Hiding it under my bed was a temporary measure. I figured I'd bury it in the woods when I went up to the cabin. How was I to know it would fall and be discovered in the hospital?"

"What about Diamond? Was he a pig, too?"

"No," she said sadly. "I liked Bob. He just got in the way."

"You made it look like a suicide," I said. "Was that your idea?"

"That was easy enough. Art told me what had happened and I figured that we'd just make Diamond the fall guy. I told Bobby I was afraid that someone was out to get me next. I made up some story about how Marcano's killer was stalking me and Bobby bought it. He really was a sweet guy. He offered me his gun and was even nice enough to load it for me. He said it would give me protection.

"When he told me about the charges Art had made against him, I talked him into going back with me to refute them. I had him call Demaret knowing that Fusco was in the office. When Art gave Fusco the phone, I pulled the trigger. Then I took off my gloves and put them on Bobby's hands."

"You don't show the least bit of remorse," I said.

"Why should I!" she snapped angrily. "It's a tough world out there. I want my piece of it. I'll do anything I have to do. When Demaret gives me my cut of the half-million, I intend to make up for a lot of lost time."

As if on cue, Demaret came back into the living room carrying two suitcases.

"Pick whichever one you want," he told her. "I split the money evenly."

"Art," she said, "don't you think I trust you? Put the blue one behind the couch, but first give me a little peek."

He opened the case. I could see pile after pile of hundreds.

"That's the money you made from drugging Marcano's stock," I said.

"Very good, Eagle. What else do you know?" Demaret said cockily.

"What I don't know is why Marcano needed you two as partners. He was the one who originally came up with the corrasalin and fentanyl scam. Or was it you, Art?"

"No, you got it right again. Marcano had been playing this tune for two years. I only came aboard the last eight or nine months. I just want you to know that I discovered how he was doing it long before you did, Ken. I tailed him to San Francisco and videotaped him making a buy of fentanyl. Then I stayed on him all the way to Seattle, where he picked up the tack needles. I figured, why the hell should I have to sweat out each new administration and each new contract year? I could make all the money I wanted by cutting myself in on Marcano's scam. I nailed Orlando, showed him the video, and told him I was going to throw the book at him. He was scared I'd take down his brother, too. The guy's a chemical whiz at Cal Tech. He's the one who hatched the whole scam. Marcano had no choice. His only out was to make me a partner. In return for his dough, I guaranteed that he wouldn't get busted. I tipped him off before every search and I ran interference for him when I injected the horses in front of everybody." Demaret laughed.

"It sounds like you had a good thing going," I said.

I wanted to keep them occupied. Courtney was looking at the money, her left hand balancing the weapon in an almost haphazard way. If I could move a little closer it might be possible to make a successful grab for the gun.

I didn't have any illusions. I was going to be the next victim. Just like Diamond, I had gotten in the way.

"Sure we had a great thing going. It was like having the key to Fort Knox, but I didn't know how bad Marcano was when it came to money. The man had to have everything! He wanted gold . . . and cars . . . and he even wanted to get involved in that breeding operation along with a group of Saudi princes and European aristocracy. The man didn't know how to stop spending. I kept telling him he was going to call attention to himself, but he was too desperate to care. I never even knew about the money he owed guys like Bath Beach."

"If he spent so much, where did this half-million come from?"

I was about to make my move when Courtney abruptly closed the case and stood up. She put the money behind the sofa and turned back to me.

"Art, bless his soul, came up with the idea. He and Orlando deposited half of their winnings in a special vault. It required two keys to get the money out. Art had one and Marcano the other," Courtney explained. "Art thought that would solve Orlando's spending sprees. Of course it didn't work."

"Come on, Courtney, we're wasting time," Demaret told her nervously.

"Relax. No one knows Ken came back here. We've got to take him upstate with us now. The later we leave, the less prying eyes around," she said.

"Why upstate?" I asked her.

Demaret and Courtney exchanged glances. I didn't have to be told this was one trip I wasn't going to return from.

"It's nice up there. You'll like it," Demaret said soothingly.

He reached over and took the gun from Courtney. "Maybe I better hold this in case he gets any ideas about jumping you."

"You think you can use it?" she asked.

She was needling him for having made her kill Marcano.

"Don't worry. If he tries anything, I'll blast him."

Courtney walked over to the front window and looked out. "This neighborhood has people walking dogs all night long. It looks pretty clear now," she said. "Let's give it another few minutes to be sure."

"Did you really recognize her from the days you were in the field, Demaret, or was that part of the bullshit story, too?"

"You've seen my memory in action. No, that was legit. I figured I could use her help."

"How?"

"Marcano had an eye for the ladies. I put them together. I'm sure you can figure out why," he said. "She's a very beautiful woman."

"Art, I didn't think you'd noticed," Courtney told him. "Maybe there's hope for you yet."

Demaret ignored her.

Courtney, at least physically, was every man's dream.

"You wanted her to get his vault key—or at least find out where Marcano kept it."

"That's right. She did a great job."

"That was good practice for you so you could steal mine," I told her.

She shrugged. "I told you I do whatever I have to. At least you were a lot more fun than Marcano."

"I'll cherish that thought in the few minutes I have left," I said bitterly.

"I'm sorry it had to be this way, but it was your choice. Too bad you didn't feel comfortable walking around without a halo. Keep him covered, Art. I'll drive my car into the driveway. Take him out the side door. We'll come back later and take care of *his* car."

She put on her coat.

"Just hurry up!" Demaret told her.

I thought about making a play for the gun in Art's hand. Unlike Courtney, he was very aware of where I was and what I might be planning.

Courtney closed the door behind her.

"Don't get any ideas, Eagle. Court's right. I couldn't kill Marcano, but that doesn't mean I won't do you. I'm not spending the rest of my life rotting away in prison."

"It's still not too late for you, Art. You didn't kill anyone. You could walk away from this."

"Save your breath," he told me. "I never walk away from a deal."

"You're trying to tell me there's honor among thieves? How long will it be before she decides that you're the one who's in the way?"

"Eagle, don't try putting ideas in my head. I've been a cop of one type or another for the past twenty-five years. You've got no cards left to deal. Just keep quiet and make it easier on all of us."

"How do you justify it to yourself, Art? How do you make the transition from FBI agent, top security man, to thief and accomplice in murder?"

Demaret laughed to himself. "Before I got involved with Marcano, I had the grand total of thirteen hundred bucks in the bank. That's what I had to show for my life, Eagle, a lousy thirteen hundred bucks. I made some bad investments, I got hit with some unexpected medical bills—but so what? A guy is supposed to be able to show more than thirteen hun-

170

dred after a lifetime of work. Marcano spent more in a week-
end than I made in a month."

"That doesn't . . ."

"I'll tell you something else. Do you know how the Racing Board was going to reward me for my years of service?
They were so pissed because I couldn't nab Marcano right
away that they were going to boot me out on my ass. How's
that, Eagle? Some twenty-four-year-old political hack was debating whether or not Art Demaret should be retained," he
said bitterly. "I had the choice of busting Marcano, getting
some favorable ink and a pat on the back, or cutting myself in
for millions."

"Why did he have to be killed?"

"He brought it on himself, dammit! We had our own
mint, Eagle. It was easier than printing money. All Marcano
had to do was lay off and slip one over maybe once every two
weeks. . . . The greedy bastard couldn't do it. He thought he
was invincible. I said, 'If they got Nixon, they can get you,
Orlando,' but he just laughed it off. No amount of money was
enough for that guy. I guess he had some kind of sickness that
compelled him to spend and spend. It was like he had a death
wish. 'Here I am, look at me.' I heard they were going to
check into his taxes. I heard that the DA's office was going to
put the squeeze on him. He just laughed it off."

"You could have walked away from him."

"Sure, just like that. I should have put my faith in some
judge who was going to make an example of me for violating
the public trust. Do you know what it means for a cop to do
time in prison? It's as much a death sentence as the chair."

"So you decided he was expendable."

"It was him or me."

"The money in the vault was an extra incentive, I suppose."

"You can't be a little bit pregnant. I was in for the whole
pot. I figured I could use Courtney to get Marcano's key. I
told her she was helping out in an investigation, but she saw
right through that. Once she got the key, she held out on me
until I agreed to cut her in."

"So you made her a partner just like that?"

"Look, Eagle. Courtney is one smart woman. She's got

brass and balls. She showed me how it could be done without getting caught."

"Yeah, I know about that," I said ruefully.

They'd needed a sucker to pin Marcano's murder on, and that dubious honor had fallen to me. Using the same wiles she had on Marcano, Courtney had managed to get my keys, make dupes, and return them without me knowing. That had given her access to my apartment where she'd taken the shirt she'd planned to use to implicate me. When she went down in the spill, it was Demaret who'd gone to my locker and taken my watch.

I'd played right into their hands when I blasted Marcano in the papers. Art knew the best time to move was right away, but he'd backed out at the last minute. Courtney hadn't let the moment pass. She went to her house to pick up the items Demaret had left for her. Then she calmly had the driver take her to Marcano's house where she'd stabbed him to death.

■ CHAPTER  We could hear the car pulling into the driveway. Demaret very carefully put on his coat and waited as I zipped up my parka.

"Come on, Eagle, move!"

The car was the box-type out of General Motors, this one from their Pontiac division. Demaret opened the rear door and I slid onto the cold backseat. Courtney was turning her head, looking around to see if anyone was watching. Demaret got in next to me and closed the door.

"You better not take the thruway or any other road that requires a toll," Demaret warned.

"I've already thought of that. I'll take route seventeen up to the cabin." Courtney sounded annoyed at his questioning of her plans.

"You really let her take over, don't you, Art?" I prodded.

"She's good at it. I don't have an ego problem."

"No, but you have all kinds of other problems. You had a

neat little money-making scam, you and Orlando. Now you've got two, and soon three, murder raps to worry about. She's done wonders for you."

"I warned you once to shut up," Demaret said dully. "Save your breath."

He was right. I was wasting my time trying to talk to him. They were accomplished, cold-blooded killers and they were sure they could pull it off.

I focused on Demaret. There was no way I could try to get the gun away from him. He never took his eyes off me and the gun always stayed pointed at the center of my chest.

There had to be something I could do, but literally for the life of me, I couldn't figure out what. I couldn't see any way out of this. They were taking me to Courtney's desolate cabin and they were going to kill me. I fought to push down the panic. *Think positively, Eagle. You can't let fear paralyze you.* I had to be ready for something to break my way.

I had once shared a stage with the coach of a pro football team. He had said that in any contest there were an average of four chance events that decided the final victor. As an example, he mentioned a fumble, with the ball squirting free and players from both teams after it, or a forward pass batted in the air with both sides having an equal shot at it. This coach had said that the team who went to the Super Bowl, on average, controlled three out of four of the "up for grabs" plays. The difference between winning teams and the rest of the league was that the players had anticipated the possibility.

What possibility could I anticipate?

I tried to come up with some scenarios. Perhaps the car would go into a skid and I could pounce on Art. Maybe Courtney would pass a light and get pulled over by a patrol car. I kept anticipating the possibilities, but the car kept tooling along at fifty-five.

Gus and Arlene had both been right about Courtney Reed. I owed my friends an apology, although, in the end, they, too, had been taken in, with Arlene even offering to defend Courtney. I remembered poor Bob Diamond. He had been completely innocent. He was what he'd appeared to be, in Courtney's terms, "a sweet man."

We were out of the city now. Taking me to the cabin in the Catskills was a good idea from their point of view. They could shoot me and bury my body in the woods without a chance of it being discovered for years. Maybe a decade from now a construction crew would come across a skull and bones and the cops would make an identification from my dental records. Until then, I'd be another Judge Crater or Jimmy Hoffa.

I knew my disappearance would spark an investigation. Courtney would swear that I had dropped her off, and that was the last time she had seen me. Demaret would offer to lend a hand in the inquiry and manage to thwart any real chance of progress. They'd get away with it, I decided.

I could even see Courtney working with Gus in a major effort to come up with clues to my disappearance. She'd stay close to Gus and use him to land my old spot with Joe Herrera's stables. Arlene would win the total acquittal of all charges against Courtney in the South and after a while, the only person who would still remember me would be my daughter, Bonnie.

Bonnie would have to grow up without a father. I would miss her wedding. I wouldn't be around to see my grandchildren born. I would have to . . . *take it easy, Eagle!!*

What the hell are you doing? Stop with the imagination and stay with facts and reality. You're not dead yet. You're sitting in a car with two very dangerous people and although things seem bleak, you've been in tough spots before and gotten through. Hang in there, Eagle. Hang in there!

I recognized the area we were going through. There was a stretch of about nine miles of straight, flat road and then we'd veer off onto the country road to the place that Courtney had rented.

It was one of those crystal-clear evenings that seem to happen after a storm. The moon was half-full and the stars were shimmering points of light. It always surprised me when I was away from the city how bright the night really was. The only time most city kids saw a sky like this was when they went to the planetarium.

Although a lot more snow had fallen upstate, the roads were completely clear. We went up Joy Road, came to the fork, and then Courtney guided the car onto the Eaton property.

"Ken, I don't know if you noticed, but there isn't another

house around here for four miles. I don't want you to get your hopes up that somebody might happen along."

"I don't have any false expectations. I know why you drove me out here."

"You didn't leave me much of a choice. Why did you have to be so damned straight arrow."

"Does it make it easier for you to think of it that way?" I asked.

"Hey, listen you two, enough of the chitchat. While you're flapping your jaws, Courtney, I'm freezing my ass off. The heat in this car doesn't make it to the back."

"Listen to him, Ken. Old Art is getting impatient. He makes it sound like he's the one who's going to have to do the dirty work. Is that it, Art? Do you want to do the honors on my friend Ken? I do have feelings for him, you know. He isn't some dog I picked up in the street."

"All right, all right."

"I'm touched," I said sarcastically.

"Just remember, if you had opened the damn clasp on the watch, we wouldn't have to be doing this," Art said grumpily.

"I shouldn't have been doing Marcano in the first place! Get him inside," she ordered.

Art carefully stepped out of the car and waited until I was in front of him. He nodded toward the house. "Come on. Get going."

No one had shoveled the walk, so Courtney blazed a trail that Art and I followed. When we got inside, she closed the door behind us.

"Stay here with him, Art."

I heard her walk into the next room, then I heard her dialing a number on the rotary phone.

"Hi, darling," she breathed. "I know it's late but I wanted to apologize for not inviting you in. That mean old headache is gone and I sure wish you were here. You must be sound asleep and it's only nine. Please call me first thing in the morning."

"Giving yourself an alibi?" I asked her when she came back.

"It's like dressing up, Ken. Sometimes it's the accessories that make the outfit."

"Now what?" Demaret asked her.

175

"I'll keep the gun on him. I want you to walk around to the back and get the shovel that's on the porch. Then come around to the car again."

Demaret walked off.

Courtney took me back outside and we waited for Demaret near the trunk of the car.

"Are you really going to kill me, Courtney?"

"What choice do I have? I've gone this far and there's no turning back."

Demaret came up behind us. He was carrying a large iron shovel.

She returned the gun to him. "Just follow me and stay close." She opened the car trunk and took out a long flashlight.

"There's a spot about four-hundred yards in. It's going to be dark once you get in the woods. That's why we'll need the light," she told Demaret.

It seemed a lot more than four-hundred yards. That was because we walked single file and very slowly. Courtney shined the light in front of her and I followed the pool it made, and Demaret followed me. In some areas, the snow had blown in two-foot drifts. In other spots, well protected by the closely spaced trees, the ground was only lightly dusted.

We came to a small natural clearing. Courtney sat herself down on a large rock and shined the light on a patch of ground in front of her.

"Start digging!" she said ominously.

Demaret handed me the shovel.

Somehow this made it worse. I had almost resolved myself to the fact that I was going to die. Digging my own grave was more than I could handle.

"What if I don't? What will you do? Kill me?" I asked her.

"If you don't dig, I sure will kill you. Before I did though, I'd make you suffer. I can put a bullet in each of your kneecaps to demonstrate that some deaths are a lot easier than others. And then Art will do the digging anyway, so what do you gain?" Courtney said cruelly.

"Give me the shovel."

"Look at it this way, Eagle. You'll build up a healthy

176

sweat." Demaret thought he was being funny. He laughed at his own line.

The ground was cold, but not frozen. After breaking through the top soil, it got easier. It might have been one hour or two, I couldn't be sure. I was now standing in a shallow grave about two feet deep. Demaret was right about one thing. As cold as it was, my clothes were wet with perspiration.

"How much more of this?" Art asked in a bored voice.

"He's got to go about another foot. The way he's slowing down, we'll be here another couple of hours. I'd spell him myself if it wasn't for this damn arm."

"Well, there's nothing wrong with my arm," Demaret said rising. He gave her the gun.

"Give me the shovel, Eagle."

I gave him the shovel and stepped out of the hole. Demaret went at the ground with hard regular strokes.

I was very tired but I knew that if I was going to have any chance at all, it would have to be while Courtney held the gun.

"Can I sit down?" I asked her, breathing heavily.

She patted the other end of the rock. "Take a load off," she told me.

As soon as I sat down, she stood up. She walked between me and the pit and then took a look over Demaret's shoulder.

"You're doing very well, Art. Maybe another ten shovelfuls and that should do it."

I counted them down as the big man scooped up the earth and deposited it on the edge of the hole. Ten . . . nine . . . eight . . . It was as if my blood was slowly, shovel by shovel, being drained from my body. Two . . . one . . .

"Okay, that's great," she told him.

He threw the last load of dirt over the edge. He started to climb out carrying the shovel in one hand.

"Hell, Art, don't bother getting out," she told him.

"What?"

The shot sounded like an explosion. In the stillness of the woods the sound was amplified, bouncing off trees and rocks and echoing like a thunder clap.

Demaret's head snapped back like it was made of elastic.

He fell backward into the grave, knocking the shovel in with him.

My mind had been miles away. The act of digging had become almost hypnotic. The killing of Demaret brought me back to reality.

"That brings it down to one little Indian," Courtney said. "Nice of Art to leave his money at my house. It makes the pickup so convenient."

"A half-million beats a quarter-million," I said drily.

"Exactly. You don't seem very surprised at the death of our friend."

"I knew you were going to get him eventually. You weren't going to let him walk away with the money if you could help it. Art should have known better. He had a great memory, all right, but not much imagination."

"He would have been a time bomb waiting to go off. It's better this way."

"How will you explain his disappearance?" I asked her.

"I don't have to explain anything. No one knows we were here. The fact that you and Demaret disappeared on the same night will surely lead to a big investigation. So what? I'll be the broken-hearted lover and I'll lead the fight to try and find out what happened to you guys. Maybe I'll even put up some of my newfound money as a reward."

"You think you have all the answers."

"I think I'm better off than you at the moment," she said smugly.

There had to be something I could do! I kept drawing blanks. Suddenly, I came up with a plan.

"Oww!" I doubled over in pain, clutching my stomach.

"Come on, Ken. What the hell are you up to?"

I put my hand in my pocket and then drew it out quickly. "I must have a muscle cramp," I groaned.

"Well, for God's sake, don't die on me over there. I need you in the grave. Damn you, *stand up!"*

I stood.

"Now get over there," she ordered.

I moved slowly and reluctantly, but I knew my only chance was to do what she wanted. I climbed into the three-foot-deep ravine. Demaret was lying at my feet. His lifeless eyes stared skyward. A bloody third eye was in the center of his forehead.

The moon was behind Courtney's head and the brown tendrils of her hair were lit by its pale light, giving her an almost supernatural appearance. She stood over me looking down at Demaret's corpse and angling the gun at the top of my skull.

"You're not going to be able to cover us up with your arm in the sling."

"I can use my left hand, Ken. That's all I need. Putting the earth back is much easier than taking it out. I can take small shovelfuls and take a lot of time. I've got the rest of my life to rest up. It was nice of you to think of me, though."

She looked around. "Where's the shovel?"

"It's under Demaret," I told her.

I'd said it too quickly. It had sounded planned.

"Is it really? Well, why don't you hand it up to me. But, Ken, hand it up *very* slowly and put it in my right hand. I'll keep the gun right on you with my good hand, so don't think you're going to try and pull some heroic stunt."

I pulled the shovel from under Demaret and slowly lifted it up to her.

"Put the handle right here in my hand," she instructed.

I held it up and watched as she grasped it. In less than a second she had collapsed to the ground—unconscious.

Jefferson and Courtney probably weighed about the same. The fentanyl in its tack needle attached by adhesive to the shovel handle had done its job well.

■ CHAPTER Somehow, I made it through the week. It was a week that found me repeating the story of what had happened to police, district attorneys, track officials, and reporters. It was a week of very little sleep and miles of pacing around the apartment.

I knew Gus was worried about me. He and Arlene made repeated visits and Gus kept asking in a nervous sort of way, "You're all right, aren't you, Ken?"

He had been with me years before. It was only natural

that he would now fear I'd look for solace in a shot glass or a fistful of pills.

I tried to reassure him that he didn't have to worry. I wasn't going back to the place I was in after my breakup with Ann. No, this time my deep sighs and blank stares were signs of introspection.

How could I have fallen in love with a woman like Courtney Reed? It seemed inconceivable now that I'd ever had feelings for a woman who could murder three of my track colleagues. What was wrong with Ken Eagle to have fallen head over heels with a killer?

"You're not being realistic," Arlene had told me. "I've seen a lot of Courtney Reeds in my time. They're crafty and very good at what they do. They have a set of rules that's very different from the set most of us live by. These people have no brakes. If they think you took their parking space, they'll shoot you to death. If their child cries too much, they'll toss the kid out the window. We make decisions and base our actions on a mindset that we think other people share. With people like Courtney, there is no normal baseline."

"Yes, but—"

"Listen, Ken," she interrupted, "we don't usually think of evil as being young, vivacious, and pretty. Our folk tales and myths are our earliest teachers. Evil is ugly trolls, witches, vampires; it's the strange and the dirty. When evil comes in a package like Courtney, it's twice as deadly because it's so unexpected."

"She took me in so easily," I said weakly.

"Welcome to the human race, Ken. The rest of us make mistakes, too." Arlene smiled. "Courtney has been a manipulator for years. It's what she does best."

"I don't want to talk about that bitch anymore," Gus said. "I got some of my own business I have to talk about. Number one, when the hell are you going to get back to work?"

I hadn't told Gus that I couldn't bring myself to go back to the track. At least not yet. There were too many memories, too many shared moments.

"I'm going to need some more time, my friend."

"You need to get to work!" Gus told me, pointing his cigar at me. "Okay, I got some more business. . . . I'm gonna marry Arlene."

"What?" I said.

"What?" Arlene chorused.

"You heard me, I'm gonna marry you," he told Kirshbaum. "You have a problem with that?"

He set his jaw belligerently.

"In the middle of a conversation, you just throw that in?" Arlene said in amazement.

"So what if I did? What do you say? Are you going to marry me or what?"

"That's not my idea of sweeping me off my feet, Gus Armando."

"Yes or no?"

"Yes," she said.

"Now I'll be romantic." Gus smiled.

He pulled a ring box out of his pocket and gave it to Arlene. She seemed to be in a state of shock as she opened the lid. It was a Gus special . . . a pear-shaped diamond cut in double-digit carats.

"My God!" Arlene gasped. "Gus, it's beautiful!"

She threw her arms around him and they sealed the engagement with a kiss.

I wanted to be happy for them. I did everything I could to show my enthusiasm but somehow my words sounded forced. Gus and Arlene's happiness just made me feel even more alienated and alone.

■ I cut myself off from the outside world. The Sullivan County real estate people were able to rent me the Eaton place, since the lady who had been occupying the premises was in some kind of legal trouble, they told me. When I gave them my name, there were raised eyebrows and hushed conversations. In the end, they let me rent the property. Why there? I wasn't sure I knew. There were plenty other places without the dreadful associations, but I needed to be there. Trial by fire? Sink or swim? For some reason, it was important to stay at the Eaton house.

I took out the phone and canceled the newspaper subscription. I told Gus it would only be for another week or so, but the weeks had now stretched to over a month.

There were the pills one of Gus's psychiatrist friends had

prescribed for me. I was assured they weren't habit-forming but I left the bottle on the table unopened. I studied the stacks of six-packs in the small town grocery store I shopped in. I knew it would just take one beer to start me on a road that I couldn't turn back from, but I bought a six-pack and a bottle of scotch anyway. But they, too, stayed on the kitchen table unopened. They watched me silently, mockingly, waiting for me to fall.

What are you doing, Eagle? What are you trying to prove?

I jogged, chopped wood, enjoyed the sights and sounds of the country. At night I watched the stars and let the heavens put everything in perspective.

■ A limousine appeared early one morning. It was a long, black stretch with a chauffeur who opened one of its doors.

My guest was Mark Russell.

"Jeez, you look like shit. What happened? You forget how to shave?" he asked me.

"It's my mountain look," I told him.

"Mountain look, huh? Whatever turns you on, kid."

He shrugged. He saw the liquor and the pills. "What the hell is this? Breakfast?"

"No, it's a challenge."

Russell stared at me. "Your agent told me you might not ride again."

"I was thinking of calling it quits."

"Rethink it!" Russell advised. "I don't know about your challenge, or your mountain look. What I do know is you and me got a deal."

"I wouldn't be any good to you on a horse."

"I'll take a shot with you. I think you're the best. I also think I got the horse that's going to win the Kentucky Derby."

"Not with me. I'm through, Mark. You want to beat me up? Kill me? Go ahead," I shrugged.

Russell ignored me. "I've got something to show you." He tossed a set of Polaroids on the table. "You tell me that's not the most beautiful animal you ever saw."

I gazed at the pictures. The horse was magnificent. It had the long neck and tapered body of a classic distance runner.

Its black coat shined with vitality and its body rippled with muscles.

"That's Ginny's Little Guy?" I asked.

"That's Ginny's Little Guy," he said proudly.

"Can he run?"

"We clocked him yesterday morning. He did a half in forty-four; and five furlongs in fifty-seven, and that's on the deep Belmont training track."

"That's race-horse time," I told him.

Was that my voice rising in excitement?

"I want you to take a look at him and let me know what you think. I want you to exercise him tomorrow morning. You in shape under all that hair?"

"I'm in great shape. I've been running, and—"

"Well, let's get the hell out of here," Russell said.

I nodded. "You really think this is a Derby horse?"

"Guaranteed!" Mark Russell said.

I followed him to the limo, looking at the Polaroid shots of the young horse who could be "any kind." Then I thought of something.

"Hey, where are you going now?" Russell called to me.

I walked back to the house and picked the items off the table. I carried them to the bathroom where I poured the beer and scotch down the toilet. Then I opened the pill bottle and tossed the contents into the bowl with the alcohol. I flushed it all away.

Outside again, I walked to the limo. I hadn't noticed before what a beautiful morning it was turning out to be.